Our Dead Bodies

Jerry Wright

Published by Trellis Publishing, 2021.

OUR DEAD BODIES

First edition. June 28, 2021.

Copyright © 2021 Jerry Wright.

ISBN: 979-8224477203

Written by Jerry Wright.

OUR DEAD BODIES

JERRY WRIGHT

The ax felt heavier in his hand than it did when he chopped wood every autumn for the winter. He knew the weight was emotional and not physical but there was still something contradictory about the ease with which it arced over his shoulder and closed the distance to the teenager's head. She didn't have a great deal of hair left, and he wondered briefly if that had anything to do with how effortlessly it seemed to cleave her skull. She crumpled to the ground in front of him. The ax didn't travel with her but her body simply slid off in a sadly anticlimactic way. He had to sidestep because his grip had loosened and the ace head swung down and toward him.

She was dead and—

Could he call her that? If the unnaturalists were right, she died weeks or even months ago. Hell, if the unnaturalists were right, the immediate guilt and self-loathing that washed over him was inappropriate and wasted emotion. He felt it, though.

She couldn't have been older than fifteen when she was... alive? He didn't quite buy the theory that the girl hadn't been alive before the ace fell. If not death, then what? Trauma, yes. Resurrection, maybe. Some kind of resurrection unlike everything promised. There was no glorious new body, no virgins, no cavorting with the gods. There was only an ace that cleaved too easily and belied the significance of the end.

He didn't know if she lived before the ace fell or if she was dead. In any case, that part of her life in which she was rational couldn't have lasted for more than fifteen years. Perhaps that part of her life ended months ago, perhaps as long as a year ago. Every part of her life was over now.

He leaned against the ace, resting the head on the ground. He wanted to wipe the blade on the grass but he couldn't come up with the energy, couldn't come up with any energy at all. She wasn't bleeding. That part of the whole mess was the most disturbing. . Somehow, the fact that blood didn't seep from her and pool around her made everything seem hopeless along with violent. It made the loathing seem contradictory as well but that didn't mitigate it at all. It seemed wrong, and he wished he could somehow make the death more visibly significant, less like killing a prop

A sudden rustling in the trees to the left of the campsite startled him and the ace instantly came back up as he whirled toward the noise. Two men stepped forward.

Men, alive in every sense.

They held shotguns, and when they saw him, the guns lowered. "You got her for us, then," one said amicably.

He let the ace return to the ground and sighed. "You were hunting her?"

"Yes," the man replied. He was short, ruddy faced, and wearing camouflage he'd probably bought from an army surplus store years before everything went to hell. The companion was thin and mousey. Images of the old cartoon with the big bulldog and the tiny terrier leaping around it in sycophantic bliss came to mind and he resisted the urge to make a comment. "Good thing you knew how to take care of business. I guess we drove her this direction." The man smiled and rolled his eyes. He shook his head and lifted his hands almost apologetically. "Her? Hell. It." He stepped forward slightly and said, "Green. Donovan Green." The man nodded to the other. "That's Sean Arcineaux."

"Hal North. Lot of them out here?" Hal was true. North was not.

"Not anymore. We patrol these parts for Spring Kettle. You from Spring Kettle?" Hal shook his head and Green continued. "Little town about eight miles down the road. About two-thousand survivors." *Survivors.* The world was mostly survivors, and towns like Spring Kettle probably only had a dozen or so to address in the first place. Hal nodded anyway and hoped he seemed impressed, raising an eyebrow slightly.

Green seemed happy. He seemed ecstatic. Hal wondered how many hours he'd prepared for the job with an energy drink in one hand and a video game console controller in the other. Green finally found his calling and Hal wondered if he were proud because it had only taken a tragedy of biblical proportions. He sighed again and nodded toward the girl's body but Green asked, "Where you from?"

"Dallas." He wasn't from Dallas. He knew, though, that Dallas had suffered more than any other city so that some neighborhoods lay in ruins. "Not sure where I'll go next."

"Spring's not a bad place."

"I'm going to head north. Got family in South Dakota." Another lie. He expounded on it. "No idea if they're still alive."

Green nodded. "Yeah. They ruined everything." It wasn't true. Humanity did. "You okay here? We only saw signs of this one but there could be more around."

"I'll be okay. My car has a full tank. I think I'll just pack up and head North."

"We'll burn the body. Otherwise it'll attract others."

Hal nodded. "I have some lighter fluid in the car."

"One day all of these fucking zombies will be dead," Green said.

Hal winced. He hated the word. Green's expression changed and Hal shook his head and said, "They destroyed everything. Hope that day comes soon."

Green nodded. "And life can go back to normal." Hal was pretty sure nothing on Earth would make Green unhappier. He didn't answer but went to the back of his car, opened the trunk, and pulled out the bottle of fluid. He saw his shogun in there and picked it up, too, pumping a round into the chamber. He paused and closed his trunk just as Green cried out, "Jesus! Look out! There are two in your car!"

Hal felt the familiar sickness crash over him as he brought the shotgun up and fired. Green's head exploded in red mist. Arcineaux screamed but Hal's second shot brought him down. Hal walked over to Green and looked down sadly on him. Most of his head was gone. This time, there was plenty of blood.

He stared at Green's body for a long time and wondered why he'd been more troubled after killing the teenager than now. He was still troubled but there was no guilt, no loathing. He turned around and opened the car door. "It's okay, Honey," he said. "You and Kaylee can come out now."

***

"We'll leave them," he said. "We just don't have time."

He waited as she nodded, an excruciatingly slow process now though the comprehension showed in her eyes immediately. He'd spent the first months fighting the urge to finish sentences or otherwise hurry the conversation along.

They weren't rotting. Not yet. Maybe they wouldn't. There were theories abounding about all of that. Of course, the unnaturalists wouldn't hear about it. To them, they would rot because they were dead and their bodies were unnatural. Others, those who held to the virus theory no matter how many times it was debunked, portrayed it all as mind over matter, as the minds convinced the bodies they were dead. Others, primarily those who debunked the virus theory, claimed it was a mutated version of leprosy, and the rotting occurred at an accelerated rate simply because of the inability to feel pain and thus address small wounds. Somehow, the bacteria caused encephalitis in some and not in others, so some became violent and some didn't.

Hal thought that last theory the most likely but it didn't account for the sudden outbreak in various geographical regions. The lack of pain was real, though. He'd seen Kaylee slice the palm of her hand on a jagged piece of metal, seen her keep playing with no indication she felt any pain at all. He'd scrubbed the wound and bound it and then taken a book on leprosy from the library, wistfully wishing the government, which undertook heroic efforts to keep certain institutions in place, would have done the same for libraries. Knowledge would certainly be lost in a generation unless the growing anarchy somehow slowed.

The books stressed something called visual surveillance of extremities, VSE, as a means to prevent rot. Evidently, the key to living with leprosy was scanning your fingers and toes constantly and by doing so catch any small cuts for treatment before they became infected. Of course, Kaylee and Lori couldn't do it themselves. That meant he had to constantly survey their extremities. It was habit now, Hal guessed, as they removed themselves from the car and helped him pack up the campsite.

They were still them.

He saw it less and less lately but they were there beneath whatever dullness the condition brought. They were there behind the strange, pinkish pupils that revealed their condition to Green and Arcineaux. They were there, and so far outside of their eyes their bodies still seemed like them. He knew they were there. Mannerisms remained that proved it, the way Lori inclined her head and sighed when Kaylee frustrated her even if the phrase "Young lady, don't make me ask again" had shortened to "Young lady, don't" in a long, low sentence that took three times as long as the original. Kaylee still climbed in his lap to say, "Please, Daddy!" even if the journey took her a minute or two and the words were barely recognizable.

The unnaturalists were winning.

They were winning and it was open season on the infected, which Hal guessed made a lot of sense to some. The violent infected behaved just like the movies, not moving like the creatures with that weird shuffle but still killing and some even eating their victims. The unnaturalists were winning but there was no distinguishing between the violent infected and those who weren't.

Hal took the bodies of the two men and placed them with the teenage girl. She'd been violent, beyond hope. At least, she'd been beyond help. He took their weapons along with their ammunition and put it all in the trunk, returning with the lighter fluid and dousing their bodies. Between the two of them, Kaylee and Lori had managed to pull the tent's spikes out of the ground. He sighed, squirted some lighter fluid on a twig, and lit it with his lighter. He dropped the makeshift match onto the bodies and, satisfied with the minor inferno that resulted, walked to help with the camp. He let them work on the tent and instead packed up the little stove and the mesh grill for the campfire. Those, too, he put in the trunk.

He considered letting them finish the tent. Even though she couldn't communicate it, he knew Lori felt bitterly disappointed when he had to help her with a simple task. He grew too worried about it, though, too concerned others would come for Green and Arcineaux. He walked to the tent and put his hand on Lori's arm. "Honey. Let me do the tent. Can you and Kaylee throw sticks and branches on the bodies?" Lori nodded, her pink pupils seemed to dilate for a moment, and then she turned and walked to Kaylee. She moved slowly, more slowly than she had before. Still, it wasn't at all like the lumbering monsters from the movies. He watched her for a moment.

She was still beautiful.

She was still beautiful and he hadn't touched her for six months.

He'd wanted to. Of course he'd wanted to. They'd been active, very active, prior to Hell descending to Earth or rising up on Earth or however the damned metaphor worked. They'd gone at it like rabbits for the first year of their marriage and still went at it for most of the pregnancy. Lori became aggressive only a few months after Kaylee was born, and they'd been rabbits again. Nine years they'd been rabbits. Now they didn't do a thing, and he didn't know if he was supposed to do something or if she would or if it hurt her or if she'd be hurt by it.

He was pretty sure she wanted it. Even with all the changes, he could sometimes catch a wistful expression on her face, the one that replaced the almost placid kind of blankness that seemed to characterize their outward emotions if not their inward. He wondered if he should just do it. They would have no trouble finding an abandoned hotel on the road and there ought to be one with adjoining rooms. He could get Kaylee occupied and just do it. She felt unattractive to him plenty of times before all this. Perhaps that was the issue. Perhaps she thought he didn't want her. He could sleep with her to reassure her.

Yeah. Of course that could all be rationalization.

When the car was packed, he used the rest of the lighter fluid to make sure the bodies and branches would keep burning. Despite all of the predictions, things weren't too hard to come by. There had been some hoarding in the beginning but when people realized not enough of society had been destroyed to upend everything, the hoarding slowed down. Production had slowed for everything, stopped for most things. Really, though, that only meant there weren't a lot of pre-packaged snack chips. Vegetables and meat were still plentiful, sold mostly from little stands rather than giant mega stores.

Why did he do that? Why did he do everything he could to pretend the end of the world hadn't come? Why did he do so much justification? *Sure, everything got blown the fuck back to the Old West but hey, all the movies acted like we'd be back in the Stone Age.* There wasn't a lot of comfort with it but it helped him keep up the hatred for the people who would kill Kaylee and Lori, the people who walked around like road warriors in a world that, if anything, had plenty of gas and water left.

"Medicine." It took Lori almost ten seconds to say the word, and though he understood what she wanted he waited until she was finished and then nodded. He wondered if it made a difference to her, him not jumping ahead but waiting. He opened the bag in the trunk and pulled out three pills for each of them. Rifampicin was a leprosy drug. He'd taken it from an abandoned pharmacy. They didn't have the other two drugs used to treat it but he knew they were all antibiotics. The other pills were just antibiotics. He had bottles full of different varieties that all ended with *cyllin*. If it all really did come down to bacteria, maybe it was helping.

Lori swallowed the pills and then made Kaylee swallow hers. Hal closed the trunk. "We should get on the road now, Honey," he said.

She nodded and got Kaylee settled. It was inefficient. Hal could have strapped in her much faster but he believed Lori needed it. When she finished, Lori closed the car door and began her slow walk to the other side. "Would you like to ride up front? If we see a car, you'll have to pretend you're sleeping."

She smiled. At least, he thought she smiled. There definitely seemed to be at least a small upturn in the corners of her mouth. He intercepted her on the way to the door and pulled her to him, holding her tightly. He felt her arms tighten on him as well and had to fight back tears. He pulled back slightly and kissed her forehead. "I love you," he whispered.

He held her through the minute or so it took her to say that she loved him too.

***

The road was lonely. It felt strange to know they would likely drive for hours without seeing another car even though humanity hadn't become devastated into little pockets of survivors like all the films. People tended to stay close, though, tended to treat everywhere outside of their particular environment as wilderness. He glanced at the gas tank. They had a quarter tank, and the dashboard told him that was good for another hundred and seventeen miles. Gas wasn't much of a problem. There were still gas stations working in the larger cities and still pipelines and refineries keeping it going. Demand had dropped dramatically, though, and he filled his tank far more often from an abandoned vehicle than at a pump.

He glanced at Lori. She sat with her eyes closed and he wondered if she did that just to make sure her limited ability to react quickly wouldn't lead to their discovery. She rarely slept anymore, perhaps an hour or two per night. He looked at the rear view mirror. Kaylee's pink eyes stared forward. She noticed him looking and took an eternity to smile. He smiled back and scanned the horizon for a place to stop. Dusk, almost.

The mountains had already given way to a long stretch of plains, the kind of Southwest stretch that meant tiny towns that abruptly changed the speed limit from seventy-five miles per hour to thirty-five. Most of those towns were empty now, citizens more comfortable in heavier pockets of population, citizens more comfortable with authorities killing the infected so they didn't have to. As though the highway itself heard him, a sign came up, advertising Honey Blossom Rock as forty-two miles away. "Ready to stop for the night, Kaylee?" he asked.

It took a long time for her to get out a reply, and it took him a moment to realize she was asking him for ice cream when they got there. He hoped there was some left in one of the stores. He said, "We'll see," and then slowed because there was a semi-truck on the side of the road up ahead. It looked like it might be from the seventies and he thought that meant there was a chance for gas rather than diesel. He could take diesel, use it for lighting fires or something along those lines but it wouldn't fuel the car. He pulled beside it and Lori wasn't sleeping because her eyes opened when the car stopped. "I'm going to see if I can fill the tank," he said.

She managed to say, "Okay," and this time it was difficult to hide his impatience because in this new world—*Brave New World*, he thought bitterly—stopping in an unfamiliar place was dangerous. He held back, though, and remained in his seat until she finished and then opened his door and stepped out. He grabbed the six foot length of rubber tubing he used for transferring fuel and started walking toward the tractor to find the gas tank. He tried but failed to keep from looking at the trailer itself with its art. A family sitting down to dinner. The paint was faded but he could see the bright and smiling face of the mother holding a roasted chicken, could see the indulgent father and the boy and girl looking hungry. Alford Meats. Making families smile since 1974.

He wondered if there was food in the back of the truck but dismissed the idea. He couldn't hear the refrigeration unit working, if the truck even had one. It was possible the truck had been abandoned here years ago anyway. The gas would be old but it would work. He made his way forward and found the tank. It was enormous, a hundred or maybe two hundred gallons in a long silverfish cylinder that seemed to be placed too close to the hitch. He found the cap and held his breath as he wiped grime from it. He sighed. Diesel fuel only. He dropped the hose onto the ground and stepped to the cab to see if anything else could be scavenged.

The roar reached him before the impact but it didn't give him a chance to avoid the attack. He was able to avoid resistance so the momentum carried him away, stumbling, from the infected man.

Woman.

He turned around and backed away as she approached. If she'd been the driver of the truck, she was about as stereotypical a female truck driver as they came. He could see through years of grime the remnants of a flannel shirt of some kind. It was stained, along with what was left of her jeans, with blood, some of it fresh. She roared again and started toward him and he realized he'd stupidly left his weapons in the car. There was no easy way to get them because the truck driver stood between Hal and the weapons. She was long dead if dead was an accurate description. Portions of her skull were visible along the side of her face and the sickly white of her jawbone stood in horrible contrast to the strangely intact gums and teeth and tongue.

She was beyond hope. He could see that. Already her eyes glinted with excitement, instinct for violence. He scanned for something, anything. Realistically, his only hope was evasion but it wasn't a false hope. Though the sick didn't really lose any of their physical speed, they lost a great deal of their dexterity, their reaction time. He dove to the ground and rolled beneath the truck. His aim was off and he felt a sickening and sharp burst of agony as something caught on his shirt and dug into his flesh before tearing away as he rolled over. He gained some time, though. The driver let out a gurgling scream and he kept rolling until he'd rolled through to the other side. He was on his feet and moving before the creature decided how to follow. He paused for only a moment before heading toward the rear of the trailer. Nine times out of ten, someone as far gone as the lady would eventually decide to run in the shortest route but the idea of crawling under the truck would be difficult for her to manage. Around the trailer would get him to the weapons while she probably still waited.

So, when she slammed into him, sending him sprawling over the sand abutment and rolling into the overgrown drainage ditch, it took a moment for him to understand what the hell had happened. He felt slickness on his face and retched as he lifted himself up and tried to understand the situation. He'd rolled into gore, rotting intestines or rotting meat or rotting something. He wiped his eyes with the back of his hand. Coyote. There was a partially eaten coyote carcass, probably the truck driver's dinner for the last few days. He retched again and then felt her again, this time wrapping her arms around him as she attacked. He rolled, primarily to get her beneath him rather than above, and then he lifted his upper body up and slammed it backward.

Of course, it was no use.

There was no pain. Or, at least, the pain was dulled so damned dramatically that there was no pain enough to shock a zombie—goddam, he hated that word—into letting go. He tried again, this time grabbing her wrists through the flannel and pulling them apart. That separated them, and he leapt up and stumbled a few feet away until he could jump over the abutment and back to the truck. He wanted to run for the car but at this point he wasn't certain he'd make it, certainly wouldn't be able to get to the weapons easily. What he needed, more than anything else, was a moment to breathe.

The cab.

He rushed to the passenger door and yanked. It was locked. He rushed around and yanked on the driver's door. It opened but as he tried to step up, he felt her arms on him again. He slammed outward with the door but it only made her slide down so she gripped his legs and he ended up holding onto the seat belt to keep from falling. These situations always left him with a curious sense of conflict. The woman was clearly beyond hope, beyond any help he could offer her. Still, he couldn't bear to think of her as anything other than a woman, as a woman who once had hopes and dreams and perhaps still did. How could he? If she were beyond hope than wasn't it just inevitable that Lori and Kaylee would be beyond hope soon?

Kaylee. Lori. Ultimately, the need to protect them overcame his hesitance and though he winced as he did it, he lifted his free leg and brought it down hard on the truck driver's shoulder. The woman grunted but didn't stop.

Woman.

Creature.

Thing.

He tried desperately to consider her a thing as he pulled his foot back and brought it down again, this time on her face. He got a gurgled scream from her but her hands still didn't relax their grip on his leg. If anything, her grip tightened and Hal felt something visceral and realized it was real fear. It was urgent fear, fear he'd lost some time ago in the omnipresent state of continual, frightened despair. He cursed himself for leaving his weapons in the car, cursed himself for an oversight that would surely kill him and more importantly leave Lori and Kaylee unprotected. He kicked her again but again it did nothing to loosen her grip. In fact, she screamed and yanked hard and he found his own grip failing and slid down the seat belt strap so that she was able to throw her arms around his waist.

Then he saw it. He cursed himself because he should have known it would be there. Didn't most truckers keep them? The butt was about a foot away but it was risky because to reach it he'd have to let go of the strap with at least one of his hands. Hell, the damned thing might not be loaded and all he'd have would be a club. He had to risk it, though, and he shouted to give himself some energy as he let go with one hand and grabbed for the gun. His hand closed around the stock beneath the trigger, and the truck driver finally won the tug of war so both of them fell backward. The gun came out with them but he couldn't keep a grip on it, and it tumbled to the left while he and the woman tumbled to the right. She lost her grip momentarily with the impact of the fall and he scrambled away but she grabbed his leg again before he could get clear.

The gun—he could see it was a shotgun now—was about three feet past his outstretched hands, and he clawed at the ground to try to close the distance. He made about six or seven inches of progress but she yanked him backward so he lost it again. He rolled over and a rock on the shoulder of the road bit into the small of his back so that he screamed as sharp pain shot through him. It angered him, and fueled by the anger he kicked out again with his free leg, catching the driver on her chin, a solid kick that sent her sprawling back. Of course, she leapt for him again but he'd gained the time he needed. When she landed on him, the shotgun was pointed at her. It ended up wedged against her midsection and he pulled the trigger.

And not a damned thing happened.

For a moment, nauseous fear gripped him. The damned thing hadn't been loaded after all but as the butt dug into his shoulder, he realized he'd never pumped the action, so he screamed again and grabbed the pump with his free hand, pulling it down and hearing a satisfying click. He still didn't know if it was loaded but he pulled the trigger. The explosion left him hurt and deaf. In the struggle, the butt of the gun had moved to his chest, and he felt like something broke from the recoil. The driver, though, flew back and landed on the ground, her midsection more like shredded rags of flesh than a body. She was screaming, Hal thought, but the sound of the gun still rang in his ears so he couldn't be sure. He got to his knees, and the movement sent shards of hurt from his chest. Bruised ribs maybe but broken ribs probably. He still had to deal with her.

Head shots always killed them. They weren't the only things that killed them but they always did the trick. He could feel a tear running down his cheek as he lifted the gun to his shoulder again. He aimed for her head and hesitated because he knew the recoil would hurt like hell. Finally, the sight of her screaming face was too much and he whispered, "I'm sorry," and pulled the trigger. The sound was distant but the pain in his side was profound, and he saw the woman's face disappear in red mist as the edges of his vision blackened. He felt the ground beneath him leap up and then felt hands on his cheeks.

He opened his eyes.

It was night. He'd been out for at least three hours. Lori held his face in her hands.

***

He watched the fire as it flickered, sending interesting shadows against the truck. It took a great deal of time but he learned from Lori he'd been out for an entire day. She'd managed, with Kaylee's help, to drive the car behind the truck. That, in and of itself was remarkable. She'd grazed the driver's side against the trailer so there was a wide gash but appearance didn't really matter anymore. She'd left him on the ground, afraid to move him, but she and Kaylee had scavenged the truck. She'd put everything she thought might be of use in a little pile. There was a first aid kit, flares, and some blankets. There were also cigarettes, and Hal smoked one now. None of the food in the trailer was good except for a case of teriyaki beef jerky. A few packages of it was boiling along with a few onions and some canned corn over the fire.

There was something both frightening and reassuring about her actions. He was pretty sure she wouldn't have been able to keep things together if he'd been dead. On the other hand, he wasn't entirely certain she knew he'd wake up. Still, she hadn't reacted with blind instinct. She'd reacted, against all odds, as the Lori before all the shit hit the fan. She'd reacted, and she and Kaylee weren't wandering the desert or declining. Kaylee slept in the car at the moment but she sat beside him, and Hal looked at her in wonder. "You did good, Lori," he said.

"Well," she said. It took a long time to get out, and he looked at her expectantly. She stared back at him and said, "Well." He waited. "Not." He still watched her, trying his best not to become impatient. "Good," she said.

It took him a moment, and then tears welled up in his eyes. Well, not good. She'd corrected his grammar. She'd corrected his grammar! He reached for her and pulled her close to him, and before he could think about it, his mouth found hers.

Six months, really closer to three quarters of a year. He felt like weeping the entire time but he didn't, and she hadn't lost any of her skill even if she'd lost some of the speed. It was slow, sweet. When he finished, he lay atop her and felt the warmth of the fire against his sides and kissed her and finally wept. She slid her hand slowly up his back until she found his head and she stroked his hair softly and kissed his neck and his cheek.

They woke in the morning and his chest felt better but Lori insisted, in her way, that they address the injury so he used a roll of cloth sports bandages to wrap his ribs tightly. When he was finished, they woke Kaylee and ate jerky stew for breakfast. Kaylee played quietly at the side of the truck as they packed the car, and when he closed the trunk, Lori said, "Thought...you...didn't...want...me...anymore." He felt tears threatening and pulled her to him.

"More than I ever have, Lori." He fought back the tears. "More than I ever have."

He held her until she let go of him and called to Kaylee. He found it interesting that the two of them had no trouble finishing each others sentences or more commonly simply reacting to what the other was attempting to say. Kaylee made her way over, and for a moment Hal didn't recognize the feeling he felt. It was hope.

He secured them in the car and turned the engine over. He backed up and saw a car in the distance behind them. "Get down," he said. They obeyed but he felt a horrible sense of foreboding anyway, and he realized the car was slowing down. "In the glove box, Lori," he whispered. He kept his eyes focused on the rear view mirror and waited until Lori pressed the gun into his hand. The car was slowing, only about twenty yards back. The headlights filled the car and he lifted up his hand to make sure they could see the gun in it.

The car slowed and then pulled up beside them. The man in the driver's seat appeared to be alone. He was Hal's age. Maybe a little older. A lot more sedentary. Probably an accountant or a middle manager before the shit hit the fan. He too held a gun. Hal pressed the button on his door to bring the window down and the man did the same with his passenger window. "I don't want any trouble," the man said. Hal didn't reply and the man said, "Any food left in the truck."

Something about the man's eyes seemed vaguely familiar. It wasn't just the fear because the fear was on everyone's face these days. There was furtiveness. He hid something. Hal brought his gun down but only so he could chamber a round discretely as he said, "No. Well, yes. There was only some beef jerky, a case of it. We only kept about half, and the rest is around the side of the trailer."

The man nodded. "Thank you. I'll drive around. I don't want trouble."

We. God damn it. *We only kept about half.* That was an inexcusable mistake but the man didn't seem to notice. He nodded again and moved his car forward and Hal sighed in relief but then saw movement in the man's backseat and lifted his gun. He thought for a moment he caught a glint of metal but then dropped his gun. It wasn't silvery or even reflected tail lights. The glint was pink. The infected ducked back down but the glint was pink. Hal realized he was shaking as the man pulled in front of the truck and turned his engine off.

Hal turned his engine off, too, took a deep breath and stepped from the car.

"Please!" the man said. "I don't want any trouble." Hal looked at the man. He stood with his gun pointed toward them but his stance was all wrong. He didn't know how to use it.

Hal lifted his hands up and said, "I'm not going to hurt you. I don't want trouble either. I just want to show you something. Please, put down the gun and come over here."

"You want me to get rid of my gun."

"No," Hal said. "You can bring it. Just stop pointing at me." The man seemed like he was lost for a moment and Hal added, "We can help each other, maybe. Please. I won't hurt you and I won't hurt whoever's in the car." It was the wrong thing to say, and the man's eyes grew wide. He shook more and Hal worried that the gun would go off whether or not the man intended it.

"Lori," Hal said. "There's someone else, someone else like you and Kaylee. Sit up."

The man's expression didn't change and Hal realized his headlights likely made it hard for the man to see. "I'm going to turn off my lights," he said.

"Don't you move!"

"I'm going to turn out my lights so you can—"

"I said don't you move! I swear to God I'll shoot you and—" The man suddenly stopped speaking and his face seemed strange for a moment, almost crumpling. His hands seemed to grow weak and Hal watched as the gun fell from them and tears welled in the man's eyes.

"My God," the man said and Hal turned to follow his gaze. Lori stood there, out of the car, pink pupils almost glowing.

***

Frank. That was what the man claimed his name was but Hal was pretty sure it was something else because he didn't respond to Frank naturally but paused as though remembering his alias whenever he was addressed. His wife was Clara, and she reacted with only the typical slowness of the infected, so Hal was pretty sure that was accurate. They hadn't stayed at the truck. It was too likely anyone passing by would stop there. Instead, they drove with Frank behind and Hal in front for about four hours until they found a private house. It was probably a farm house before, and Hal led the tiny convoy down the private road to the location. More accurately, they drove down the private road down six empty stockyards and through several hills until Frank caught a glimpse of something that appeared to be a chimney and turned to investigate. The house lay in a small valley. Of course, the house was abandoned. However, Hal found goats grazing in the backyard, shot one, and thanked God for 4H years before as he butchered it. He brought the meat inside and discovered the stove still worked, which meant the place ran on propane and not municipal gas. He set the meat to simmering and then went out back again to shoot two more goats.

Frank approached him while he was skinning them. "We can't stay together for very long," Hal said. "You make it riskier for me and I make it riskier for you. But, these goats will give us each some meat for a day or so."

"Where are you going?"

"Away." He didn't mean it as a deflection. It was the only answer he had.

"I... I heard there was somewhere we could go." The man paused. So did Hal. He looked at Frank and raised an eyebrow. "I heard there's a hospital from when it first happened, and there are still doctors there and, well, they're just past the border."

"Mexico?"

"No, Canada."

"Quebec?" The French separatists in Quebec had finally gotten their wish while the world was falling down around them. They were a separate entity. Of course, most of Canada was anarchy now. The U.S. had fallen into a structure almost like city states. Canada had done the same but not giant cities like Toronto but an endless sea of smaller settlements.

"No. What used to be British Columbia, I think. It might be on our side of the border, though."

Hal sighed. "How do you know it's not just a goose chase?"

Frank shook his head. "I don't. It probably is but what the hell else am I supposed to do?"

"I don't think we can go there together. Washington and Oregon were hit hard but they're all survivalists there, the only hope of getting through there is by being less, not more, obvious."

Frank looked hopeless, and Hal felt horrible but he added, "This is too cliché anyway. Here we are in the end of the world but there's some city of refuge our heroes can escape to? That's every goddam apocalypse movie ever made."

Surprisingly, Frank didn't back down. "Maybe you're right. Maybe it is cliché. But that might be why there's a shot. Maybe someone thought about it, set it up."

Hal sighed. "I don't think there's any hope for it but even having a destination has got to be better than what we have going on now." He was pretty sure he wouldn't be heading that direction, pretty sure Frank wasn't careful enough. The best solution was to find somewhere in the mountains, far enough from civilization that they could live without fear of discovery, somewhere with game and fresh water. Sure, the family would live like they were settlers in the 1800s but he was pretty sure they could live a fine life there until some scientist somewhere discovered a cure.

He'd been raised on a small farm, and he'd hunted year round, his father not particularly concerned with the seasons and their farm remote enough that it didn't matter. Somewhere along the way they'd procure more ammunition and some livestock, maybe some seed to get started. It would be a hard life but it would be a good life. It would be a hell of a lot better than life as it was now. He didn't want the confrontation now. Already, Frank seemed too needy. They'd develop two routes to the supposed hospital in Canada and then Hal just wouldn't show up. It was the best course of action.

Best course of action.

He felt oppressive guilt pushing down on him. Jesus. Best course of action? He looked at Frank and then stood up. "We should stick together," he said. Frank looked surprised. "It's riskier in a lot of ways but neither of us have as much of a chance alone." He paused and then added. "I don't think there's a hospital but we can find somewhere, pick up supplies along the way and start a life somewhere. We'll head that direction but let's not tell them we're heading toward a cure."

"They don't deserve hope?"

The words hurt. Hal sighed and said, "They deserve hope, hope for what's possible." He started to walk away but instead sat back down. "But they don't deserve to be disappointed again when it doesn't happen."

Frank looked like he was going to reply but then his wife stepped onto the backyard carrying a bottle. It took a moment to see what it was. Whiskey, Irish whiskey. Hal raised an eyebrow. Clearly, at the end of the world, the most important issues were food, shelter, and water. Nevertheless, he hadn't found it all that surprising that the first thing that disappeared with all the looting was the booze. The beer and wine followed shortly thereafter. You could run across a bottle of beer or wine now and again but it was all but unheard of to find the good stuff. Sure, people made homemade brews and there was always shine available but it wasn't grain based and was risky and likely laced.

Lori followed Frank's wife, and she held two cups in her hands. She handed them to Frank. Frank's wife had to adjust her plans so it took her a moment to change course and hand the bottle to Hal. He thanked her and realized he didn't know her name. "Frank," he said. "My wife's name is Lori. My daughter is Kaylee."

Frank said, "She's not my wife. I mean, she is but we never made it official. I call her my wife and she calls me her husband but I had a modest inheritance, a trust fund back in college. We would have lost the income if I were married. So... well, we never got around to making it official even though it's been... God. Why the hell didn't I just take her to the courthouse and..."

His voice trailed off and Hal took a breath. "Things aren't over, Frank. You can still marry her."

Hal watched Clara bend over toward Frank. Clara, damn it. Her name was Clara. "Clara." The woman slowly pulled away from Frank and Hal said, "I remember your name now."

It took a while for her to smile but she did. Then, she tried to speak. Hal was patient but Frank seemed embarrassed. He started to say something but Hal held up a hand. "I read somewhere that when someone stutters or has a stroke you can't finish for them. I know this isn't the same thing but maybe it feels the same way for Clara." Frank nodded and Hal quickly added, "Or for Lori or Kaylee."

Clara tried again and after an eternity got out the word *more*. Frank and Hal waited but she was done and she was smiling. Frank asked softly, "More what?"

Lori answered. "Bar," she said. "Whole bar." Hal thought she spoke more quickly than she had in a while and he smiled broadly. She smiled back. Clara smiled as well. They seemed proud about their discovery, and Hal wondered at a world thrown back a hundred years or more where nonetheless, the discovery of spirits was a fabulous thing.

He smiled at the two of them. "Do you two want to get glasses?" Lori looked surprised and he said, "I think it will be fine. No interactions with the drugs and alcohol isn't going to spread any infection." He smiled again. "Just one glass, though." Lori took Clara's hand. He watched them slowly walk away and found it strange they could move with excitement but still move so slowly.

"You think it's an infection, then?"

Hal shrugged. "I think I want my wife to feel normal." He finished skinning the second goat and said, "Can you see if there's a shovel or something? We should bury the skins and the entrails. Just in case there are any of them around."

Frank nodded and stood. By the time he returned, the wives were back with glasses. Hal stood and said, "Frank and I need to clean up. How about you pour the drinks." He purposely didn't open the bottle and took Frank a short distance away, dragging the skins and the entrails atop them with him. Frank dug and Hal said, "Lori likes to do things even if it takes a long time. I think she's getting faster, too."

"She's getting better?"

Hal nodded. "Yeah, I think so. Use it or lose it, maybe."

***

By the time they finished with the two new skins and the one from earlier, the women had glasses full and waiting. Everyone also had a plate of stewed goat and Kaylee ate inside. Hal sat next to Lori and kissed her cheek. Frank seemed surprised but he leaned over and kissed Clara as well. Hal saw movement and panic welled up for a moment but it was Kaylee, stepping closer and then making her slow way to Hal and Lori. He kissed her cheek as well and said, "It's time for bed, little one." She groaned but then simply lay at his feet and closed her eyes. He smiled and shrugged and then took a sip of his whiskey.

Heaven.

Jesus. How long had it been? He drank bourbon, sometimes Tennessee, but he didn't like Irish whiskey. It just didn't go down as smoothly as bourbon. Hate was probably too strong a term but he'd skipped the hard stuff altogether if his preference wasn't available.

But it tasted like Heaven nonetheless. It burned nicely going down and he savored it but then noticed the carcasses of the goats on the porch. "We'll have to limit it to one drink until we can get those processed. I think we might have to smoke them."

Lori touched his hand and he turned his head. She took a long time to form words but she finally managed to say, "RV."

Hal nodded and said, "We don't have it anymore, Honey. We..." He trailed off because he was almost... it sure as hell seemed like she rolled her eyes. She smiled a half smile, a smile closer to one of her sardonic smiles from before. He suddenly wanted her again and he breathed in sharply. He fought back the emotions, though, and said. "Here. You mean there's an RV here." She nodded slowly. "Where?"

She shrugged. It took a long time to figure out exactly what expression she tried to make but she shrugged. "Did you see an RV?" Hal asked.

Her response came slowly but she said, "Clara."

Frank turned to Clara. "Did you see an RV?"

Clara shook her head slowly and then said, "Come, follow...Nathan."

Nathan. Frank was Nathan. Hal smiled but didn't say anything. Frank looked ashamed and then said, "Nathan is my middle name. What did she mean?"

Hal said, "Ask her. She's still Clara, Nathan."

He turned to his wife. "What do you mean?"

Clara stood and motioned for him to follow. Frank stood and so did Hal. Lori smiled and said, "Kaylee." She didn't stand. Hal nodded and kissed her cheek. Clara turned around and began her slow walk back into the house. She led them through the kitchen and into a small adjoining room. The adjoining room had the bar, a beautiful oak bar someone sank a great deal of money into. He paused and looked behind it. Mostly glassware but five more bottles of Irish whiskey were in an open box. He saw a few mixers, a bottle of gin, and a half-open bottle of vodka.

He put the gin in the empty slot in the case of whiskey and lifted it to the top of the bar. Lori stared disapprovingly at him, and he was almost too shocked by her ability to create the expression to protest. "Alcohol is antiseptic," he said. "We may drink a little bit for special occasions but this is for medicine." He was almost certain she rolled her eyes again but she did it with a smile. He sighed. "Clara, please show me the RV."

He followed slowly behind the women as Clara walked to a door, opened it, and then stepped out of the way. She took a great deal of time to gesture for him to look inside but he waited patiently. Lori was very far advanced compared to Clara. Perhaps Clara was simply advanced in the disease. He didn't know. He nodded to her and stepped inside the room.

It was a pantry, and it was remarkable because the pantry was full. There were canned goods as well as pasta and beans in canisters embossed with roses and grapes. There was even hot chocolate in a tin, and he wondered why nobody had looted the house. In fact, the house seemed pretty damned intact altogether, and that made no sense at all. He turned back to Clara and said, "This is good, really good. Why did you say RV, though?"

She lifted her hand and Hal realized she was pointing. He'd grown accustomed to waiting for Lori or Kaylee to finish their words and gestures so the impatience that hit him suddenly was unexpected. He held on even though he had to clench his teeth to do so and when she stopped moving her hand he looked where she pointed. On the top shelf were RV supplies. There were cans of toilet treatment, rolls of tissue designed for portable toilets, and a few other odds and ends. There were also batteries, large batteries he assumed handled the RV auxiliary power. Clara hadn't seen an RV. She'd seen evidence of one. That was inductive reasoning. That was remarkable.

He turned. "This is a great discovery. The RV might be here and we'll have to search the property. On the other hand, the people who lived here might have been traveling when... well, when everything happened." Both women nodded and he made it official. Lori only took about two-thirds of the time to complete the affirmation as Clara took. He smiled and said, "Why don't we finish our drinks and in the morning we can try to find the RV?"

She nodded, and Hal thought perhaps she nodded more quickly than she had before.

***

He made love to Lori again, this time in a king sized bed under dusty blankets but blankets still. He felt normal, and though he thought perhaps it was better because they'd broken the ice by the truck he suspected it was more than that. She was better. She'd been awkward before, physically awkward. She didn't move like some kind of porn star now but she moved a hell of a lot faster than she had before. By the truck, she was like a virgin experiencing things for the first awkward time. Now, she was like a 1970s European soft core actress, moving slowly and gently but still actively participating. He held tightly to her afterward and then rolled over and she put one leg over him and her head on his shoulder.

Like before.

Like before everything.

He stroked her back and realized she was crying softly. He lifted her head and kissed her. "We're going to get through this," he said. "We will." She kissed him, on his mouth, and though it still took a while, she told him she loved him.

She rolled off and though she was slow, she was still faster than before. He was certain of it. He watched her walk to the walk-in closet and open it. Kaylee lay there sleeping. Was it activity that did it? Was it like physical therapy? Maybe they could never get rid of the pink eyes but was it really something as simple as using it or losing it? He chuckled softly and Lori turned to look at him. He didn't tell her he was considering marathon sex sessions as treatment. Instead, he told her he loved her and he was happy and that someday they would find a house like this where they could try to be normal. She smiled and came back to bed.

In the morning, he was surprised to find Clara up and excited. Frank/Nathan was still asleep. Lori walked to Clara and hugged her, and Hal wondered if there was some kind of secret language the two shared. Did all of the infected share a language? He wondered why they didn't attack each other, the ones who were far gone with the condition. He'd always assumed there was something in the disease, some pheromone or something. With the way the two interacted, though, he thought perhaps there was more. Finally, Lori let go and walked to Hank. Her expressions were definitely clearer. Were they? Was he too hopeful?

She kissed him and said, "She found it." He waited but that was it. She'd said the words and there was almost no delay. She seemed like she was on the brink of laughing at his shocked expression and she kissed him again. Her second sentence took much longer to get out. "Hurry before her boss wakes up."

He nodded and started toward Clara but then stopped. "Boss?"

Clara looked a little embarrassed but from behind him, Lori giggled and it actually almost sounded like a giggle. He turned to look at her and the smile that greeted him was almost mischievous.

***

The RV was a class C. They'd rented one every summer before Kaylee and then one week a year. This was a newer model. It was in something that looked like a barn, and it was hooked up, still plugged in and still connected to the sewer drain. Hal tried the driver's door. It worked. The keys hung from the visor. He recognized the ignition keys but he also recognized the keys to all of the compartments along the side as well as the side door. He grabbed them and walked around. The side door was unlocked so he didn't have to use the key. When he opened the door, a step slid out with an electric whirring sound. There was still power. He stepped inside. The thing was clean. Perfectly clean.

Except for the dust.

There weren't any cobwebs but he could smell cedar and mothballs. He imagined the owners were in their fifties before everything fell apart. He imagined the husband was an engineer or something, someone who worked off checklists. Even the dust wasn't that bad. He surveyed things. The stove was propane rather than electric. That was good. There was a bunk above the cab. A couch. It became a bed. The dining area sat four or five and it collapsed into a bed as well. He walked past the refrigerator and saw the shower and the bathroom. Good working order, it appeared. He opened the door beyond them and stared in at the master room. Again, it was very well kept. Only dust.

Hall walked back out and tested the engine. Worked. He went back outside and opened each compartment in turn. The RV was stocked will all of the RV essentials. Flares, tool kit, first aid kit, spare bulbs, spare fuses. He was particularly happy to find a solar switch right next to the propane tanks. He climbed underneath. The propane tank was detachable. That was good. It was still fairly common to come across standard propane tanks with gas. It was near to impossible to find anywhere to fill them. He climbed into the driver's seat and turned the key. He didn't know why he found it so surprising that the RV worked but it worked. He saw there were two tanks and saw the thing ran on diesel. That would actually make things easier. There were far more abandoned trucks than cars. The gauge showed a full tank. He flipped a switch above it and the gauge fell to two-thirds of a tank. Two tanks. Good to know.

He turned off the engine and said, "Your boss?"

Clara looked embarrassed again and Hal realized she was probably twenty years younger than Frank. "Are you safe with him?" She nodded her head vigorously or at least as vigorously as she could and Hal nodded. "Okay. We have some work to do. Why don't you two and Kaylee see about cleaning this up and then packing up the food and the supplies. He thought a moment and then said, "Hold on." He drove forward and out of the barn. He turned off the engine again and then climbed out. He walked several yards away and caught the glint of panels on the roof. He made his way back, opened the compartment, and toggled the switch that initiated the solar power. Then, he climbed back into the RV and held his breath as he reached for a light switch.

It worked.

He sat down on the couch and tried to figure out how to handle things. He sure as hell wasn't going to let Frank or Nathan or whatever the hell his name was drive the RV but that meant leaving his car behind and he wasn't inclined to give up his car. It was a stupid vanity, sure, but it was still there. He sighed and considered just taking Lori and Kaylee and leaving. He wanted to take Clara, too, imagined what it had to be like. The girl was probably in her very early twenties. She was probably eighteen or nineteen before she became infected, and that meant the asshole had been fucking a girl who was all but a child.

Jesus. Was he just keeping her around for the guaranteed lay?

He felt bile rising in his throat and leapt from the couch and out of the RV, retching horribly as he shot partially digested goat onto the grass. He stumbled farther away from the RV and that was when he saw the glint of metal against the side of the barn. He made his way over and then stopped a few yards away. There were two of them, obviously the owners of the RV. They screamed when they saw him and stretched their hands toward him but they were pinned down. Their throats had deteriorated enough that their screams were no more than raspy whispers.

He stepped closer. It was hard to see exactly what had fallen on them but it looked like machined steel. A closer look told him it was almost like part of the frame of a pre-fabricated steel building. They were four or five yards from the side of the barn. He looked up. There were more of the steel frames on the roof of the barn. He still couldn't see how it had worked to pin them but thought perhaps they'd climbed on the roof or something like that and fallen...no. It didn't make sense. They were too old to climb. More likely an animal climbed on the roof at the wrong moment and a poorly balanced stack shifted.

They were pinned opposite each other, and that made the situation even more tragic. Each had torn the flesh from the others legs. A goat skeleton lay next to the man as well. Hal sighed and reached for his gun.

Damn.

He made his way back toward the house and into the bedroom where he'd slept. He reached for the duffel bag but stopped when he saw movement. "I'm sorry," Frank/Nathan said. "But I'm taking the RV. I'm taking it with Clara." Hal turned his head slowly. The man had Hal's gun.

"Does Clara know about this?"

"Wake up. Clara doesn't know anything. None of them do." The man gestured with the gun. Hal wasn't sure if he knew how to use it but the man seemed comfortable with it in his hand. "We're with walking vegetables. That's it. They're good for pussy and nothing else." He paused and his smile almost made Hal sick again. "Good pussy, though. The best. They spread their legs when you tell them to and they don't argue with you afterward. You know, Clara was a huge problem before all this happened. Now she knows her place."

"Was she going to tell your wife, Frank?"

The man's eyes narrowed. Hal knew he'd hit a nerve but the man replied evenly. "Right now, you and your pets get to live. We'll take the RV and the supplies and we'll leave. You want to change that? You want me to put a bullet in your brain and have more than one pair of docile legs to spread whenever I want?"

His instinct was to leap up and attack but Hal fought down the urge. Then, he saw Clara in the doorway. He took a deep breath. "Don't you love Clara?"

The man laughed. "Love? That was all she wanted before this shit happened. Look, I loved the way she could move her body, I'll give you that. I loved that I could do anything, anything at all. If my wife didn't give it to me, Clara would. Sure, she's more like some fucking plastic blow up doll now but that's better than nothing."

"Don't you give a damn about how she feels?"

"How she feels? Grow up. Jesus. Listen up, Boy Scout. I really care about how she feels when I'm screwing her. How's that?" Clara's eyes were sad, not quite filled with tears but sad. Hal watched her step away and to cover the noise he stood up. Immediately, Frank trained the gun on him and said, "What the hell do you think you're doing?"

Hal lifted his hands. "I want to go downstairs and get you keys so you can leave." He wanted to add how much Frank sickened him but he didn't. "Unless you want to try them yourself," he said.

Frank eyed him narrowly and said, "Okay. Let's go." Hal walked carefully past him and out of the bedroom. The man walked behind him, making his steps obvious, making sure Hal knew he was there.

"Is it Frank or is it Nathan?"

"What?"

"Your real name. Which is it?"

"Why the hell does that matter anymore?"

Hal shrugged. It didn't matter, not really. "Were you in love with your wife before this happened?"

"You talk too much."

"What if they can still think? What if they can still feel?" It was a pretty damned stupid question, really. The man didn't give a damn about her thoughts and her feelings before.

"Have you ever had an affair?"

"No."

There was a pause. They were near the door to the backyard now, and Hal could almost see the expression on Frank's face in the glass door. It was indecision. "You know," Hal began but the man interrupted him.

"When you're married your wife has expectations all the time. Then some beautiful young girl shows up at your office and she adores you, she wants you without all those expectations. You don't have to prove anything to her. You don't have to be anything than older and her boss for her to love everything about you."

Hal reached the door. "It's not too late to give her a real reason to love you."

"Just get the keys, and don't try anything."

Hal slid the door open and stepped out. He walked to the RV, moving slowly in the hopes a brilliant plan would spring to mind but nothing came. He could take Frank, Nathan. He could take whatever the hell his name was but he wasn't sure he could do it without a wound and he wasn't confident he could keep that wound from pushing him into sepsis. "Listen. This is a bad choice—"

"Just shut up! This is happening and you can either live with it or die right here."

He sighed again and made walked to the driver side door. He opened it and pulled down the visor. The keys were gone. "You already took the keys?"

"What? What the hell are you talking about?"

He turned to face him. "What kind of game are you playing? The keys are already gone."

Frank looked nervous, frightened. "I may not be the kind of guy who stars in blockbusters but I have the goddam gun and I'll use it." Hal wasn't certain if he'd really use it but he was certain the man had no morality left.

"I don't have them. They're gone."

"I will kill your daughter and then your—"

"Hid... them..." Hal turned to see Clara. She had her arm up and pointed at Hal. She repeated the words and an eternity passed as she did. Lori and Kaylee stood next to her, looking scared.

Frank/Nathan smiled and walked toward them. "You're going to tell me where you hid the damned keys or you can just say goodbye to one of them. Which one Hal? You want to say goodbye to your already dead wife or your already dead daughter?" He shouted the last words and raised the gun. Hal prepared to leap toward him as his heart raced but Clara stepped in front of her ex-boss.

"You...don't...love...me?"

Frank lifted up his hands. "Of course I do," he said sweetly. "I'm doing all of this for you."

"Heard... talk... him."

"Darling," he said. "Anything you heard I only said because he's dangerous. That's why I need the keys, to get away from him." He lifted his arm and pointed the gun at Kaylee. "You have three seconds, Hal." Hal prepared to attack but Clara put her hand on Frank's wrist.

"I... know... hid... them..."

Frank smiled and the smile grew malicious as he turned to Hal and said, "See. She knows her place." He gestured with the gun and Hal followed the direction until he stood next to Lori and Kaylee. Frank turned his attention back to Clara. "Where did you see him hide them?"

"No... I... hid..."

Something was wrong. Hal didn't know what it was but Lori wasn't afraid. She was sad. He was pretty sure she was sad. It was possible he misinterpreted her expression but he didn't think so. He'd seen that expression time and time again. Lori wasn't afraid.

Kaylee was.

Kaylee was afraid. She held tightly to Lori's hand and stared at her father expectantly. She expected something from him, something miraculous. Hal wondered for a moment why he still found it so difficult to accept his daughter's disappointment, even now when life itself was nothing but disappointment. He sighed and said, "You can still stop this, Frank."

"You don't know anything," the man said. "My name isn't Nathan or Frank. That was my company."

"Frank and Nathan's? The video stores?" Hal tried to remember the press releases. The places would be out of business but they kept their adult choices long after the larger chains bowed to pressure. Then, abruptly, the firm announced some kind of accounting problems. Hal shook his head. "The infection was the only thing that kept you out of prison."

"Like this isn't prison?" The man's eyes narrowed. "Now give me the keys."

"I don't know where they are."

"I... know..."

The man nodded. "Get something to tie him to the RV." Clara looked around in confusion and the man snapped, "Rope damn it. Get some God damned rope or something." The girl jumped (as much as someone in her condition could) and then went to the RV, opening one of the side compartments and rummaging around. That just didn't make sense.

Didn't make sense?

That was bullshit.

She wouldn't have thought to look there. What the hell was going on? He turned to look at Clara but couldn't see anything of note. He turned to look at Lori. She still looked sad but there was definitely no fear. Clara stood up.

Christ.

She had a gun, a shotgun. It wasn't one of Hal's, and Hal hadn't seen it with Frank/Nathan's things. It wasn't too surprising that there'd be a gun on property in this part of the country or really in any part of the country in a home so secluded but it was surprising Clara found it instead of Hal.

"Not..." Clara began as she pointed the gun at Frank/Nathan. "Not..."

"Steal," Lori said.

Clara nodded slowly. "Yes. Not steal RV."

Frank looked incredulous and Hal understood. Were they getting better or were they always better? Were their minds just stiff, needing stretching? It was impossible. None of it made sense.

Except the guns.

They made far too much sense.

Frank/Nathan's face remained incredulous for a moment and Hal looked back at Clara. He doubted she'd ever used a gun in real life. He knew Lori hadn't. The shotgun was a pump shotgun and from the state of the RV, Hal doubted the man who'd owned it was the type to leave a shell in the chamber. He looked back at Frank and watched his face grow angry. The man trained the gun on Clara, murder evident in his expression.

"Wait," Hal said softly. "I know where the keys are."

"No!" He turned to look at Lori. She hadn't managed that level of intensity in her voice for a very long time.

"Where are they?"

"I'll show you," Hal said.

He wasn't certain what the hell he was going. All he knew for certain was that if the situation remained as it was Frank would fire and it was likely Clara would die. It might be too much of a stretch for Frank to accept that Lori and Clara had collaborated on the little insurrection but the risk was too high. He had to get the man to follow him and somehow find an opportunity to get the gun away from him.

He'd have to kill him.

Hal felt horrible about it but there wasn't any choice. He had to kill him. The man would always be a threat and he'd be a greater threat in close quarters. He turned to Clara. "Lower the gun, Clara."

"No." He thought for a moment her eyes glinted with tears.

"Please, Clara," he said. "It will be okay. We'll all be okay." It seemed to take forever but the barrel of the shotgun finally came down.

"Show me," Frank said. Hal walked around the front of the RV with no real idea where he planned to go and caught movement in the distance. He paused and stared. There were dozens of them. Maybe tens of dozens. "What the hell are those?" Frank asked.

"Goats," Hal said.

"Then why the hell is there grass? That many goats would have decimated this place. It should be dirt."

Hal shrugged. It was a good question. There was no reason for the goats to leave... Hal sighed. "The keys are this way," he said as he walked into the grass and then turned toward the barn. He walked and counted the steps. Frank spoke about five steps sooner than he'd expected him to.

"Wait!" Hal stopped and turned. Frank looked at him narrowly. "You think you're so damned smart, don't you. You have a gun stashed? Hung the keys up next to keys? You want the harem to yourself, you asshole?"

Hall shook his head sadly. "There's no gun."

"Bullshit. Where are the keys?" Hal sighed, shook his head sadly one more time, turned and pointed. Frank smirked slightly and said, "Okay. You move toward the left for me. I'm going to walk ahead but this gun will be on you the whole time. Don't get any ideas or I won't just take the damned RV. I'll put a god damned bullet in your head and leave you right where it's parked."

Hal didn't reply. He sighed and stepped to the left and then watched as the man stepped next to him, moving at a slight angle so the gun remained trained on Hal's body. Now was the time. A quick strike with his leg to the knee would incapacitate him, and if he got a shot off it would go wide, very wide. Nothing about the man was physically imposing. A quick kick and a quick follow up with his fist would incapacitate him, eliminate the threat, and diffuse the entire situation. The kick would take less than a second.

He didn't kick him. Instead, he walked along sadly. "There's still time to stop all this," he said softly. Frank stopped and turned fully toward him. There was just a little bit of uncertainty in his eyes. That was enough. A quick fist to his throat would incapacitate him with no real damage. A simple motion, really. A step forward, putting his weight on his right leg and a straight jab to ensure he hit the throat and not the side of the next. Frank would probably drop the gun but it wouldn't matter if he didn't. He'd be useless. He'd be utterly useless.

Hal desperately wanted to jab at his throat. All morality suggested he should but he didn't. Frank walked backward, the gun trained on Hal and he scowled. "You'd like that, right? We all go our merry way and I spend every second wondering when you're going to shoot me in the back of the head. That's what this is all about, you just waiting for the chance. You're lucky I don't just kill you. It's mercy to let you live. You'd never do it for me." Hal stopped moving. Frank stopped as well but then smiled. "Don't you dare try anything." He kept the gun trained on Hal before he turned around.

Before he turned around and screamed.

Before he turned around and the female put her teeth into his calf and tore a chunk of it out. The gun fell to the ground and bounced slightly. Hal felt a wave of guilt as Frank lunged for it, succeeding only in falling to the ground and making it possible for the male to get to his arm as the man screamed and flailed about impotently. Frank screamed primal screams, wordless screams.

Panicked screams.

Hal might have been able to save him before the male got involved. He couldn't now. He couldn't even offer him a release from the pain. The gun was too close to the two infected. He wanted to shoot him, to give him that mercy but the gun was too close. He stared, though he desperately wanted to look away. He stared and considered it penance that he should watch a man eaten alive, a man murdered by Hal.

Murder?

Self-defense?

There was no rationalizing it, as much as he wanted to. He'd consciously decided to kill him, consciously decided to do so with the husband and wife zombies who themselves deserved the mercy of permanent darkness. He looked at Frank. The man beat at the male eating his arm but he couldn't have much strength left. Anything he gained from adrenaline was counteracted by the loss of blood. Already, the woman had a large portion of his calf stripped from the bone so that sickly white mingled with the red and black gore.

He could chance the gun. He could move in, grab it, back off, and put a bullet in Frank's head. Perhaps that would be the only thing that allowed him to sleep soundly ever again. It was too close. The male might be distracted by his meal but Hal couldn't risk it. If he were killed, or even hurt, the chances for Lori and Kaylee grew slight and that wasn't acceptable. There was no choice but to—

His ears seemed to explode with pain as he watched Frank's head disappear into red vapor. He turned, a little deaf, and saw Clara holding the shotgun. He wasn't certain if he'd ever experienced such profound gratitude and profound guilt at the same time. Surprise, too. She'd known how to chamber a round, perhaps even how to load the gun. Frank didn't scream anymore but the meal continued and he held out his hand. Clara seemed relieved to give him the weapon. He trained it on the male and then the female, awarding peace to the two of them but still leaving images in his head he knew would linger. He looked at Clara. Her expression was unreadable.

"Sorry," she said. Hal didn't know if she said it to apologize to him or to Frank.

"I'll bury him," he said.

She nodded and said, "Them... too."

"Yes," he said. "Can you, can you go back to the RV? Can you make sure Lori and Kaylee know you're fine, know I'm fine?" She nodded again and seemed grateful for a purpose as she walked away. Hal leaned against the side of the barn and slowly slid to a seated position, holding his head in his hands.

***

"Why don't we stay?" It was early, and Hal opened his eyes to see Lori staring back at him. She seemed normal again, normal but for the pink pupils. She seemed normal and he was certain there'd been no hesitation in her voice.

"What did you say?"

"Why don't we stay?" He sat up and stared at her. The bodies were buried and buried deeply. He'd done it unnecessarily, really. He'd dug deep for his own benefit, to make the task somehow more meaningful, more profound. He hadn't done it to keep the bodies from attracting other infected but it would have the same effect nonetheless. He'd finished and somehow leaving didn't make sense and they all ended up remaining for one more night.

One more.

"What if he was right, Lori?" he asked. "What if there's a place in Canada where they're trying to find a cure. What if there's a safe haven."

"He was a liar." Again, her voice came so naturally, so perfectly that he felt a flood of sudden and desperate desire for her. He reached for her and pulled her to him, kissing her deeply. They made love, and this time without the almost overwhelming urgency they'd shared at the side of the road by the truck. Instead, he explored her slowly and wept when they finished so she held him and stroked his hair as he faded to sleep again. He awoke to the smell of coffee. He'd need to start rationing things.

He made his way down and to the kitchen. Lori sat at the table and smiled at him. "Why don't we stay?" she asked again as she got up and walked to the coffee pot. She poured him a mug and handed it to him. "Why don't we stay?"

He looked out the sliding glass window and saw Clara playing with Kaylee. Even happy, Kaylee always had a haunted look but it didn't seem to be there at the moment. Surely it was his eyes and not her expression but he didn't mind. "What if there's a haven out there?"

"Here is a haven."

He smiled but kept his eyes on Kaylee. "Is Clara okay?"

She didn't reply so he turned to look at her. "Here is a haven," she repeated.

It was secluded. There were goats that would last for some time, perpetually if he managed the stock and bred them. He could probably get a garden working. They could always leave later. They could keep the RV stocked and ready to go at a moment's notice. On the other hand, they could likely gather others to the place.

"Here is a haven," she said insistently.

"I suppose it is," he said. Lori reached over and put her hand over his, squeezing gently.

OUR LIVING FUNERAL by Chelsey Baker

The heavy, beige colored subway doors closed with a definitive thud. Riley sat perfectly still in her seat, feeling the momentum of the train move her body as it slowly picked up speed again, careening down the track she couldn't see. Her green eyes wandered until she could see her mother's shoulders in her periphery, mere inches away from her own. Nancy had on a floral blouse with cut out shoulders. Riley could see her mother's tan skin slightly sway as the subway rushed forward under the Chicago streets. Since the divorce, Riley's mother had begun to dress like a woman half her age.

Nancy stared down at the grungy brown floor of the train. All she could see was a myriad of shoes and a piece of foil from a gum wrapper. She wiggled her feet, watching the overhead light shine off of her red toenails. Her eyes wandered to her daughter's shoes beside her. She wore dingy black Chuck Taylors. A hole had begun to form near one of the soles.

"You need new shoes," Nancy said quietly.

Riley glanced down at her feet. "These are fine," she replied.

"Fine? There's a hole in your right one."

Riley sighed, staring at the fake happy people that smiled down at her from the advertisements that lined the ceiling of the train car. There were so many things, a litany of things, she could argue with her mother about. Her shoes felt too easy as the subject.

"I'll get new ones, alright?" Riley said and scratched her cropped brown hair.

Nancy hated when Riley moved her arms about. She always tried to look away, but it felt as though her eyes were magnetic and couldn't help but stare at the crooks of her daughter's elbows. A series of red sores and bruises covered her daughter's pale, sallow looking skin. Most had scabbed over but they still looked angry, defiant almost. It felt as though each little sore looked back at Nancy, mocking her.

"You didn't have a long sleeved shirt to wear?"

Riley turned her neck to look at her mother. Her light brown eyes were steely as she gazed back. Fine lines surrounded the corners of Nancy's lips. Riley had the same slightly upturned nose as her mother, but it was the only thing that looked familiar. It was the only thing they shared.

"I'm sorry that my addiction embarrasses you," Riley snapped through gritted teeth.

She didn't bother to keep her voice down. An elderly man with thick round glasses glanced at her before blinking and turning his head away.

It had only been four hours since Riley had been kicked out of the Gateway Alcohol and Drug Treatment Center, but she absorbed her mother's shame as though it were her favorite sweater. It was familiar.

"I'm not embarrassed," Nancy snapped, running a hand through her shoulder length brown hair. "I just... Don't like to see what you've done to your body."

Silence reigned. Mother and daughter listened as the train clicked and whirred along the track. Their bodies swayed slightly as the subway shifted upward, barreling up from underground towards Belmont.

Riley watched as trees suddenly appeared on either side of the murky windows, brown and green blurs that lined the two story brownstones, built in rows along the track.

Her thoughts meandered to Gateway, and the way the woman at the front desk looked at her as she was being escorted out by security. She pictured the joint, all wrinkled and burnt, that her counselor had found in her room. It was just to take the edge off—the dive and plummet of withdrawal that had her body in a vice grip. But all they had seen was a rule broken.

Nancy sighed, feeling the subtle ache of a headache begin to form in the center of her forehead. Her thoughts were also on Gateway, and the conversation she had with Tim before she had driven to pick up her daughter.

"Jesus, she got kicked out again?" her ex-husband had complained on the phone. "How could you let this happen?"

She had hung up on him, but his words clung to the air around her like smoke. How could you let this happen? They were divorced and Riley's addiction to heroin still caused them to argue. It felt like their marriage had died the moment their daughter put a needle to her flesh.

Nancy rubbed her temples, glancing at the people around them. The man with the thick glasses that sat across from them had dozed off, his head tilted back against the wall. A heavy set woman with bushy blonde hair read a romance novel beside him. To the right was a middle aged Asian man frowning as he stared down at his phone.

A cough rang out. Nancy followed the sound to the other side of the train, where a balding man sat in the corner. His skin was pasty and slightly shiny with sweat. He sat hunched in a dark green jacket, gazing at the floor.

Nancy's stomach lurched and she forced herself to look away. The man looked how Riley did whenever she stopped using. Those days where her daughter shivered and said she was ready to be done with heroin for good. How many times had those words left her lips? How many times did Nancy have to endure hearing them, knowing they were false?

The train began to slow as it approached a stop. The dozing man opened his eyes, and got to his feet with a soft groan. The woman with the romance novel glanced up at him as she turned a page. The heavy subway doors slid open and the man trudged off. A young woman with a purple backpack walked onto the train, her tennis shoes squeaking slightly as she turned left and sat in an empty seat across from the coughing man.

The doors came to a close, and everyone leaned to the right as the train began to move. Riley felt her stomach drop slightly as the tracks began to dip down, hurling underground again. The train grew darker as it sunk into a tunnel.

The sickly looking man began to cough again, his body heaving with the effort. Nancy found herself unable to take her eyes off him. It wasn't just the germs he spread with his incessant coughing, there was something about his eyes that looked strange, though she couldn't quite put her finger on it.

As she watched him, the man slowly rose unsteadily to his feet. His eyes were dazed as he stared at the sticky brown floor of the L train. He opened his mouth and a low, almost guttural sound emanated from his pale lips.

"What the—" Riley began when the man suddenly turned to his right and lunged at the young woman with the purple backpack.

The woman stared up in horror as the man opened his mouth wide and bit into her neck with a sickening, sepulchral noise. He tore into her flesh. Nancy and Riley watched in horror and leapt from their seats, as the other train goers cried out and screamed. There were eight people total, including the sick man. All of them flew over seats and down the aisle way.

All but one.

The heavy set blonde woman trembled in her seat, her brown eyes wide with shock as she watched the sick man continue to devour the young woman. Her hazel eyes were turned toward the ceiling, but they could no longer see.

Riley and her mother stood with the others on the opposite side of the train. There were five of them total. The middle aged Asian man who had been on his phone clutched at his heart through his shirt, breathing heavily. A teenaged girl cried in the corner, her heavy black eyeliner ran down her face. Between the two was a muscular black man with a gold earring. Riley stared at the blonde woman, her fingers still clutching the pages of her romance novel in her seat.

"MOVE!" Riley bellowed.

Her voice was loud and frantic. The sick man looked up from the young woman's corpse, his face covered in her blood. His eyes, which seemed to have turned slightly yellow, shifted from Riley to the blonde lady. He growled, shoving the dead woman aside as though she were a rag doll, and stood upright. His gaze seemed hazy and unfocused. Nancy got the distinct impression that the man, whoever he was, was no longer fully there. His movements were clumsy, uncoordinated, and his expression was vacant. She wondered if he had lost all cognitive function.

The passengers on the train watched as the sick man charge forward just as the blonde woman did. She tossed herself from her seat, but her heavy body made her slow. The sick man squealed and jumped onto the woman's back.

She cried out as her legs buckled underneath his weight. Before her head hit the ground, he had already dug his teeth into the side of her neck. Blood gushed onto the floor of the train as he made contact with her carotid artery.

"No!" shrieked the teen, frantically shaking her head. Her dyed black hair flew about her face as she stared at the growing pool of blood on the floor.

"Quiet!" the black man snapped, glaring at her. "You'll attract its attention."

"Oh," Riley said and pushed between the two. Behind them was a metal door with a square window in the center. Below the window, in bold red letters read STOP DO NOT OPEN EMERGENCY USE ONLY.

Riley grabbed the silver handle and jerked it to the left, hearing the gears shift. She opened the door and waved at her mother and the others. "Into the next car!" she urged.

The Asian man was the first to run through, followed by the black man. He had grabbed the teenager's hand and pulled her after him. Nancy looked at her daughter with an appalled expression, then walked over the threshold.

The next car only had two people in it. One was a red haired man with clusters of freckles all over his face. He immediately stood up, watching as everyone piled in with a bemused expression. The other passenger was a middle aged woman with beautiful olive toned skin.

"What the hell is going on?" the red haired man demanded, looking at each of them.

"We don't know, this man just started attacking people!" the teenaged girl blubbered. She touched the metal spikes on her choker nervously.

"It's alright," the black man said, staring into their former car through the window. "The door is locked; he can't get to us."

Nancy stepped around the group and walked to the right wall of the train. Halfway up was a metal box that jutted out from the wall. On the left side was a speaker and a small silver button. "I'm gonna call the conductor," she said, and pressed the button down with her index finger.

"Hello?" Nancy said into the speaker. "There is an emergency! A man is attacking people! The police need to be called!"

Her request was met with a few moments of static and then nothing.

"Hello?!" she yelled. "Can anybody fucking hear me?!"

The teenager sobbed and sank into a seat. The Asian man sat beside her, blinking over and over again. Riley wondered if he was in shock.

"Is anybody getting service?" the black man asked, frowning down at the phone in his hand.

One by one each Chicagoan whipped out their phones and shook their heads. There were many sections of the L where nobody got service. They were underground, beneath several layers of metal and concrete.

"What do we do? What do we do?" the teenager asked, her pale, skinny body trembling.

"We should keep moving," the Asian man said, his voice soft but certain. "We should put as much distance between us and that man as humanly possible."

The black man shook his head, absentmindedly touching his moustache. "I disagree. I think we should stay here and make sure that the man doesn't go anywhere or hurts anyone else," he reasoned. "He could easily go through the other emergency door the opposite way."

The olive skinned woman quietly came forward to stand with the others. "You say he has hurt people?" she said with an accent Riley could not quite place.

"Not just hurt, he killed them!" the gothic teen said as black makeup continued to cascade down her face.

"Perhaps we should kill him? It'd be self-defense," the foreign woman reasoned, shrugging her shoulders. She wore a quartz necklace that made a soft tinkling sound as she moved.

"Whoa, whoa, whoa, I'm not killing anyone!" said the red haired man, jabbing his thumb into his mustard colored sweater. "For all I know you guys are the crazy ones!"

The black man took a step forward, glaring into his face. "All you need to do is look through that god damn window to know we aren't crazy," he snarled.

"Get out of my face!" the red haired man barked and pushed his palms against the man's chest.

Within seconds, the black man grabbed him by the collar of his sweater and shoved him. Surprised, the red haired man stumbled backwards, tripping on his own feet. His body fell into the emergency door, his head making contact with the window with a sharp crack.

Nancy flung herself between the two of them with her arms stretched out and her palms up. "Hey!" she snapped angrily. "Attacking each other is going to get us nowhere!"

The red haired man rubbed at the back of his head, a scowl on his face. The black man took a deep breath then looked down at Nancy with a curt nod.

"Okay," he said, breathing out. "Okay."

Riley ran a hand through her cropped brown hair, trying desperately not to think about getting high. Such a situation would tempt any addict, she was sure.

"Maybe we should move to the next car?" she suggested. "I doubt all of the intercoms are broken, and if we can contact the conductor, he can reach out to the police."

The Asian man nodded his head vigorously in agreement, but the black man frowned down at the ground.

"I think if we were to keep moving, panic would spread. You saw what happened to that woman when she was paralyzed with fear," he reasoned, crossing his arms across his muscular chest. "I think as long as we know where the man is, we should remain here."

"I don't want to die...," murmured the teen girl, her black hair falling around her face as she stared mournfully into her lap.

"Nobody else is fucking dying, alright?" Riley growled. "That man, whatever happened to him, looks messed up in the head."

"Well, obviously—"the black man interjected.

"No, I meant that he doesn't seem to be high functioning anymore," Riley said, cutting him off. "I don't know what happened, but I think the cognitive parts of his brain aren't working."

Nancy blinked at Riley, surprised to hear her very own thoughts come out of her daughter's mouth.

"I agree," Nancy murmured—which made Riley look surprised in turn.

"Well, that's great and all, but what are we going to do?" snapped the freckled man.

Suddenly, the emergency door on the opposite side of the train was opened and a blonde man, who appeared to be in his forties, poked his head into the car.

"Everything alright?" he asked. "We've been hearing a lot of yelling," he pointed behind him with his thumb.

The Asian man shook his head while the teen visibly shivered.

"No, man," said the black man with a grimace. "A man has started attacking and eating people. We have him isolated in the next car. Seems to be some kind of virus or infection."

The blonde man blinked at him. Riley could see his Adam's apple bob nervously above his teal colored necktie. "He's.... eating people?" he repeated, just barely above a whisper.

"Yes," Nancy nodded. "And we've been trying to contact—"

But the blonde man had shut the door with a definitive slam. Riley and Nancy watched, their jaws flying open, as the man locked the door behind him. He continued to look through the window, his expression a mixture of sorrow and resolve.

"Hey!" the black man growled, reaching the door in a couple of strides. He pounded his fist against the wall, staring at the blonde man as if he could kill him with his eyes.

"Open the door!" he demanded.

The blonde man stared back, his mouth turned down at the corners. He slowly shook his head. "I'm sorry," he mouthed. "Not safe."

The teen stared at the man from his seat, her blue eyes wide with fear. "Oh my god, we're gonna die!" she wailed and began to cry with renewed fury.

Hesitantly, the Asian man slowly moved his arm around the girl's shoulder, patting her awkwardly. To his surprise, she turned into his embrace, resting her head into the crook of his neck.

"Hopefully they contact the conductor in that car," Riley said, still staring at the blonde man. He had the decency to look sheepish as they made eye contact.

The black man slammed his fist against the door again, then turned his back to it. He sat down in the nearest seat and rested his elbows on his legs. He shook his head over and over again.

Nancy sighed, trying to suppress the rising panic she felt deep in her gut. "Okay," she said to herself. "Okay, let's think..."

She began to pace in a small circle on the brown floor of the train. Everyone was quiet apart from the teen, who continued to sob into the Asian man's shoulder.

The red haired man, who had been leaning against the wall with his arms crossed, suddenly lifted an index finger. "What if we pull the emergency brake? The conductor will instantly be notified that something is wrong," he said.

Riley shook her head, scratching at her skin. "The emergency brake should only be pulled when we are beside a platform," she argued. "If we pull the brake now, we will be stuck in this tunnel and police won't be able to reach us."

Nancy frowned up at the ceiling. Above the sound of the teenager's sobs, she heard a faint tinkling sound, like the first sprinkling of rain on a window. The train was still underground, enveloped in a tunnel of concrete.

The teen opened her mouth to speak, but Nancy shushed her, holding her hand up in the air. "Hold on," she said. "Do you guys hear that noise? What is that?"

Everyone sat still, their eyes unfocused as they concentrated on the sound.

"Where is that coming from?" Riley asked, looking out the window behind her.

Within seconds the noise became louder. Nancy and the other passengers watched in horror as pieces of glass fell from the cracked window of the emergency window. The sick man had somehow realized that the window had been broken, and was trying to crawl through.

"Ahh!" the Asian man cried and stood up from his seat. He grabbed onto the teen's black lacy shirt and pulled her with him towards the other end of the car as she screamed.

Within seconds, the black man was back on his feet, frantically rapping his knuckles against the emergency door the blonde man had gone through. "Open up!" he cried. "The man is coming in, open up!"

The passengers of the train looked at him and then to the blonde man. He sat in the first seat beside the emergency door, adjusting the collar of his shirt nervously. He was shaking his head, speaking to his fellow passengers. None of them looked happy, but they each nodded their heads, keeping their gaze down at the ceiling.

They weren't willing to risk their own lives to save anyone else.

"What do we do? What do we do?" asked the olive skinned woman, clutching at the seat in front of her with white knuckles.

"I...I'll try to take care of it," said the red haired man. He fished into the pocket of his jeans and pulled out a Swiss army knife.

The sick man had already burrowed through the window, seemingly not concerned that shards of glass were digging into his skin as he crawled through and fell to the floor head first. He growled and stood up again, looking at the passengers of the train with a hungry look in his eyes.

The red haired man clutched at his small knife and took a deep breath. With a noise of resolve, he ran forward, raising the knife up high above his head in a striking motion.

The freckled man sunk the knife deep into the man's neck as he bent forward, sinking his teeth into his forearm. Blood began to spurt from the knife wound, but the sick man still didn't seem to notice. He used the weight of his body to pull the red haired man down the ground. Hearing the man's screams made bile rise in Riley's throat.

Nancy took the steps to go from one side of the train to the other, hovering beside the black man. "You're the strongest one here, do you think you can break one of the side windows with your feet? We could get onto the roof!"

The man nodded and turned, raising his right black boot towards his waist. He gritted his teeth together as he kicked out against the glass over and over again.

"Oh god," the teenaged girl said, watching the red haired man scream and struggle against the sick man's mouth. She bent over and vomited on the floor at her feet.

Riley stared at the knife, which still protruded from the sick man's neck as he continued to attack the freckled man. "Everyone, pull out anything and everything in your pockets and bags that could be used as a weapon" she ordered.

Nancy looked down at her purse, surprised to see that it was still securely on her shoulders. She dug into the soft brown leather, feeling around until her fingers felt the long metal nail file she always kept in there.

The goth teen took off her spiked collar and wrapped it around her fingers so the spikes faced outward.

Riley had never liked purses, and typically carried her ID and phone in her jeans. She felt the outsides of her pockets, but the only thing she had on her person was a blue Bic lighter.

The overhead lights shut off as the passengers continued to search through their belongings. There were small yellow colored lights every few feet in the tunnel, but the car was mostly dark.

Nancy peered through the darkness, watching as the sick man continue to ingest the freckled man. His victim had stopped moving and making noise...

She let out a noise of despair and turned her attention back to the black man, who grunted as he thrust his boot against the window over and over again.

"Hurry!" she begged him, frantically waving her arms.

"I am!" he growled and thrust his foot against the window. The glass finally gave way. It broke into several pieces, some of which fell into the train while others fell out onto the tunnel. Riley could hear some of the shards crunch underneath the tracks of the train cars.

"Okay," she told herself and ran to where her mother stood. With deft fingers she snatched the nail file out of her mother's hand and held it as though it were a knife.

"Help everyone through the window," Riley yelled to her. "I'll take the rear."

Nancy shook her head, staring at her daughter by the faint yellow glow. "Absolutely not," she said.

"There's no time to argue, just do it!" Riley screamed back. She waved at everyone toward the very back of the car.

The black man was already halfway through the window, slowly raising his body up, careful not to scrape himself against the rough cement walls of the subway.

The Asian man helped keep the teen steady as they stood in front of the broken window. The woman with the olive toned skin had her hands out by the frame, prepared to help the black man in case he lost his balance. Nancy watched as his torso disappeared, then his thighs. All that was left on the frame were his worn black boots.

"Once I get up there, I will reach down and help everyone up!" he bellowed to the passengers below him.

He laid his body flat against the metal frame of the L train. The roof had thin grooves etched into the metal, but they weren't deep enough for the man to hold onto. He stared down the tunnel, trying to grip the train as it began to go around a sharp bend. Despite his strength, he could not find a good handhold on the metal.

"Shiiiiiiiit!" he cried, as his body began to slip sideways. He dug his fingernails into the metal but they were sweaty and betrayed him.

Nancy, Riley, and the other passengers stared in terror as the watched the black man's boots reappear, dangling from the roof of the train. They all tried to reach out for him, but the train swiftly turned, and his body moved with the momentum.

With one last agonizing cry, the black man lost his grip entirely and flew through the air. Gravity pulled him down until he tumbled onto the tracks...and was pulverized underneath the car that immediately followed.

"NOOO!" the teenaged girl shrieked, shaking her fists into the air as fresh tears careened down her pale cheeks.

"Oh my god," Nancy murmured as she poked her head out of the broken window. Blood was smeared along the bottom of the next car. Her stomach lurched and she forced herself to look away.

Inside the train, the sick man seemed to be tiring of his meal. Riley stared at his face, studying the way his eyes continued to yellow, and his skin seemed to go grey. "Guys, I think he's turning into a zombie," she murmured.

The Asian man gawked at her from beside the window. "Impossible," he said. "Zombies do not exist."

Riley watched as the sick man licked at the puddle of blood that had grown underneath the freckled man's body. "I think they do now," she said.

The woman with the olive toned skin walked to the nearest seat and set her black purse down. She rifled through it until she said "Aha!" and pulled out a crumpled piece of paper and a pen. In capital letters she wrote INFECTED MAN, PEOPLE DYING, PLEASE LET US IN. Once she was done, she tossed the pen over her shoulder and marched to the emergency door.

"Hey!" she yelled, and slammed the piece of paper against the window.

Nancy could make out a few people on the train from where she stood. The blonde man continued to sit in the chair closest to the door. He read the sign and swallowed again. Someone must have said something behind him because he turned in his chair and moved his arms about as though he were arguing.

The passengers watched as the pedestrians of the other car gestured wildly, and debated. Riley felt dread creep up her body from the tips of her toes as she tried to read their lips. If it had been her, she would have been at that door in the span of two seconds, cranking it open, saving lives.

It seemed that some people on the train felt the very same. They pointed at the sign, visible tears in their eyes as they yelled at the man in the suit.

After a few minutes of this, the blonde man moved his arms up and down as if to calm everyone. He spoke for a few minutes and then people began to raise their hands.

They were voting.

Nancy tried to count the hands, but it hardly mattered. She couldn't tell which hands voted for what. What was sickening was how close both rounds seemed to be...

The blonde man finished counting and nodded his head. He reached into the pocket of his dark grey suit and pulled out his cell phone. He worked his fingers on the screen then brought the phone over to the window. He had it open to a text message which read,

SORRY U GUYS COULD BE CONTAGIOUS TOO. MORE DEATH.

The teen lurched forward and vomited again, splattering her shiny black Doc Martens.

Fed up, Riley walked to the door. She stared at the blonde man, wishing—not for the first time in her life—that she could set fire by sheer will alone. His mouth was grim, but his eyes were guarded, almost steely as he looked back.

He did not want this to happen to them. But he was not willing to risk his own life to save anyone else's, either.

Riley slowly raised both hands and stuck her middle fingers up. If she was going to die, she was going to die without whimpering.

She was going to die fighting.

Suddenly, her mother was beside her, pulling her arms back down. Riley was about to snarl at her, but she looked up at Nancy's face and knew her mother wasn't trying to chastise her. Nancy's eyes were wide but steady as she looked down at her daughter.

"I just wanted to tell you that I love you," she murmured, gently putting a hand underneath Riley's chin.

"I... I never meant for anything like this to happen," Riley whispered back, feeling tears begin to well at the bottom of her eyes.

Nancy looked into her daughter's green eyes, and knew what she meant. She meant that she never meant to get addicted to heroin. She never meant to cause problems for her family.

She had never meant to cause any of them pain.

"I know," Nancy said, forcing her mouth into a weak smile. "I know."

A strange gurgling sound caused everyone to look at the opposite end of the train. The zombie was staring up at them from the meager remains of the red haired man—some fragments of his sweater and a pile of bloody, half eaten organs.

The zombie gurgled again. Blood oozed from the corners of his mouth, down onto his chin. His eyes were neon yellow in color, and no longer contained any semblance of human emotion in their irises.

With mechanical movements, the zombie steadily rose to his feet. His eyes trailed from one passenger to another, looking at each as though they were a dish laid out on the dinner table. He stepped through the remains of the corpse, intent on selecting his next victim.

The passengers huddled together at the other end of the train. The woman with olive skin began to pound her fists against the window, tears streaming down her cheeks as she begged them to open the door.

The teen girl whispered a prayer under her breath, her eyes closed. The Asian man stood beside her, muttering under his breath in Vietnamese.

It seemed that everyone was giving up.

Riley gritted her teeth and walked to the broken window. Carefully she grabbed the largest shard of glass she could find. It looked almost like a thunderbolt, narrowing to a sharp point at one end. She could feel its edges bite into her palm, but she just took a deep breath and gripped it all the more tightly.

She turned to look at her mother.

"I don't think we can take him on alone, but we if work together...."

Nancy sucked in a deep breath, and looked from the zombie down to the shard of glass clutched in her daughter's hand.

"No matter what, I am not getting off this train without you," Riley insisted vehemently. "Either we work together and try to kill him, or we die trying. We die together."

Nancy looked at the resolve in her daughter's eyes and felt a tear spill down her right cheek. She didn't want to die, but as she faced her potential—likely inevitable end—she was surprised to find she was not afraid. Her tears were for her daughter, for her courage, for her selflessness. She saw a layer of depth and beauty she had never noticed before, etched into the planes of her daughter's face.

At last Nancy nodded, brushing at her tears with an impatient hand. "Together," she said.

And she, too, grabbed a large shard of glass.

They resolved to flank the zombie, hoping having two people approach him would cause him to remain unsure and unfocused. Riley felt as though her heart would leap up her chest and out of her throat at any moment, it pounded so furiously.

As she stepped forward, a fraction of her brain imagined how things would have pained out if she had had heroin coursing through her veins at the time of the first attack. She would have been dead. She would have been killed and eaten and her mother would have had to have watched it all.

I'm never getting high again, she told herself.

"Where should we strike first?" Nancy asked. She tried to keep her voice steady as she walked forward.

"Let's gouge his eyes out first," Riley said. "We will have the advantage if he can't see."

She saw her mother nod in her periphery.

"On three?" Riley said, looking to her mother. She forced her mouth into a smile, one last attempt at bravado.

"On three," Nancy repeated.

"1... 2... 3!" Mother and daughter said in unison and raced forward, holding the glass high above their heads.

The zombie growled, clumsily bringing his arms forward. His sickly yellow eyes darted between both of them, seemingly unsure as to who to attack first. It was this hesitation that Riley had been banking on. She cried out as she lunged forward, and swung her arm forward. She used the momentum to gather power behind her strike and thrust the glass deep into the man's left pupil.

On the right, Nancy was doing the same thing. She wasn't as physically strong as her daughter, so she twirled in a tight circle, swinging her arm out wide to strike against the zombie. The glass sunk into his iris with a nauseating noise.

The zombie howled in pain, taking several steps backward as he frantically waved his arms about. He recognized that he was in pain, but seemed incapable of removing the glass from his eyes.

"Now, let's grab them back out and strike him!" Riley cried out. Blood ebbed from her hand as she grappled the glass, but she did not register the pain. Adrenaline coursed through every vein in her body.

Mother and daughter held onto their shards and repeatedly stabbed them into the sallow, grey flesh of the zombie's body. They struck at his heart and chest over and over again as he shrieked in agony. His stab wounds grew and spread as they worked, until it became one huge, gaping wound above his ribcage.

The zombie faltered, his bloody eyes turned toward the ceiling as he began to sway in place. Riley extended one of her black Chuck Taylor's and kicked the man until he fell to the ground. His limbs spread out half-hazardly across the brown floor, unmoving.

Nancy stared down at the zombie, her eyes wide, unable to process what had happened. Beside her, Riley fished into the back pocket of her jeans and pulled out the blue Bic lighter.

"For good measure," she said and cranked the metal wheel. She placed the flame against the man's clothing until it caught fire.

"Look! We are approaching a platform!" the teen girl said, pointing out the window to the left hand side. Sure enough, Nancy could see the platform careening ever closer.

"Hit the emergency brake!" she ordered, pointing at the red lever beside the main entry doors to the train.

The Asian man leapt forward and grabbed the lever, pulling it with both hands until it gave way.

As the train came to a screeching halt, Riley felt her mother's arms come around her in a hard embrace. Riley smiled, flinging her arms around her mother's shoulders in turn. They were together and they were alive.

END

DEAD EYES by Ashley Waymon

Sunrise – the time of day when all the nightmarish atrocities of the world disappear like they were just figments of a teenage girl's imagination. The time of day where running from a horde of blood crazed lunatics seems far-fetched and completely bogus. The time of day where even the most feverish mind can take a step back and think, yes, the world is a beautiful and righteous place.

Mac wasn't prone to such bullshit, though. Oh no, she had learned early on in the game that stopping to smell the flowers and appreciate a pretty sunrise was the easiest way to get your legs caught in a stiff's teeth. *Never let 'em outta your sight,* her dad had always said. She intended to follow that bit of advice until the cows came home. In fact, she intended to follow every bit of advice Lt. Harry Wilson had ever given her.

The early morning air was nice and cool on her face as her feet hit the pavement. She'd camped out on a second story the night before. *Doors barred, instant street access if you need it, Mackey.* She wanted to write down all the survival gems her dad had given her over the last few months, maybe even give it a catchy title like *How to stiff a stiff* or *Lt. Harry Wilson's guide to avoiding death.* It was something she kept her mind busy with late at night when she heard scratching at the door, or when she waited behind a dumpster until she heard those god awful guttural noises they made pass into a different alleyway.

At present there were no stiffs prowling about in the street below, so she found it as good a time as any to be on her merry way. Her cherry red Doc Martens (a size too big, but who cared when the world was ending) were the perfect shoes for stealthy morning walks – they were quiet *and* properly attached to her feet. No tripping allowed in this part of town. And this part of town was *bleak.* The first reports on the news which mentioned the word *zombie* were some two months ago. Mac was surprised by the rate at which everything had gone to complete and utter shit after that. Her dad had said that society would survive this.

"Mackey," he said as he loaded up their SUV with water canisters, "civilization is too mighty a foe to conquer, you'll see."

Well, she did see. And what she was seeing as she walked the dusty debris-laden streets of Tallahassee wasn't a victorious civilization. It was a shit hole. Cars were parked in the street at all angles, some with their doors open. Others were still housing their owners now eternally clawing at the windows as she walked past.

"Want me to crack a window?" she asked as she walked past a particularly swollen looking woman snapping her teeth at the glass. The string of pearls around her neck looked about ready to snap, and Mac wasn't left disappointed. All the excitement of seeing breakfast walk past her Chevrolet prison caused the stiff to wriggle around like an eel in a bucket, providing that final bit of strain on the necklace, sending pearls bouncing off against the closed window and into the stiff's lap.

"Better get those fixed," Mac snorted and moved on.

She knew they were dead. She wasn't talking to them to reach their souls or whatever. She wasn't stupid. She was just tired of having no one to talk to. She hadn't been popular in school and preferred books to people, so it wasn't like she was a recovering socialite. But after spending her thirteenth birthday alone on the roof of K-Mart, she felt like it was time to start making conversation, even if they weren't talking back. She didn't know if Lt. Harry Wilson would agree. He was iffy on the subject of other people. One thing he had said as they drove through a small town somewhere east of San Francisco was, "People need other people. That's why we're going to Orlando. There are people there. Not stiffs, Mackey, but *real* people. They've made a stand. They have a type of barrier which keeps the dead out. Grammy and Bill are there."

She had no idea how her dad had known that her grandparents were in Orlando. At the time she filed it under *Stuff Lt. Harry Wilson knows through his divine knowledge of pretty much everything.* Mac felt something run down her cheek and wiped it away instinctively. Her fingers were wet when she looked at them. She had cried so much over the last two weeks that she wasn't even aware of it happening anymore. She sniffed and lifted her chin higher, daring her eyes to shed one more bloody tear.

She was hot and sweaty by the time she spotted a convenience store looking a little less menacing in the glare of the sun. The map her dad had left her put her on the eastern outskirts of Tallahassee. They'd come a long way from San Francisco, on a journey which would have only taken about three days to complete had they kept their SUV and not run into a million obstacles on the way. She was alone now, and the moving was slow. But if she kept to the road she could probably reach Orlando in a week or so.

Her backpack was alarmingly light as she set it down next to her on the floor of the convenience store called Stop 'n Go – exactly what she intended to do straight after she had a little browse. She went into Lt. Harry Wilson mode without giving it much thought.

Be quiet. They're not hiding from you – you're hiding from them. One thing you can count on is that the sons of bitches won't be stealthy. They make a lotta noise, and if you're quiet, you can hear them comin' before they get a whiff of you.

Mac sat down on her haunches and waited, the door directly behind her if she needed to make a quick exit. The smell in the store was a sickening combination of rotting meat and expired produce. She hadn't made a lot of noise coming in, but if anything had heard her, it would be making its way down one of the aisles towards the sound. They were attracted to sound like moths to a flame. She knew that all too well.

It was a small store with six aisles, and she could easily see the freezer lined back wall.

Don't get cocky. Just cos you can't hear them, doesn't mean they're not there. Secure the place one aisle at a time.

Slowly and quietly she walked to the wall on her left, taking care to avoid any of the broken glass scattered on the tiles.

Watch your feet.

She cast a quick glance behind the cashier's counter and stopped dead in her tracks. A shotgun was lying on the floor in a mess of putrefying body parts. The previous owner had died with the gun in his hand – virtually the only part of his body not clawed and chewed at. It hadn't been an easy death, that much was obvious.

Make a note of anything you can use, but don't get comfortable. Secure the building before raiding it.

The far left aisle was clear of both the dead and anything useful. She didn't need shampoo or toilet paper, it would only weigh down her backpack and give the stiffs something to smell. Her stomach agreed in a sudden fit of gurgles. She retraced her steps back to the front of the store.

There's no point in walkin' the store like you're killin' time, Mackey. Stay close to the exit. Your eyes know what they're lookin' for.

The second aisle's shelves were not so disappointing. Dried beans, sugar, and macaroni were strewn across the floor. She saw a few discarded cans lodged underneath the metal shelf, and made another mental note. The rest of the store was empty. No stiffs, and no buffet of hamburgers and ice cream. A girl could dream.

Mac quickly made her way to the cans she had seen, her Docs crunching over the sugar and macaroni on the floor. She studied her plunder: Old El Paso Jalapeno slices, Green Giant whole kernel sweet corn, Bush's Best Boston recipe baked beans, Campbell's Chunky New England clam chowder and a cracked bottle of Smuck's sweet orange marmalade leaking its contents onto her hand.

Take what you can, and get out. Don't burden yourself with anythin' you can't carry off easily. If you have to run, drop everything, and haul ass. Your life is worth more than a can o' beans.

She was busy stuffing the cans into her backpack when she heard a door creak. Her breath caught in her throat as she went completely still. A dragging sound came from the far right corner of the store, and with it, the ragged choking sound reserved for the living dead. Mac glanced towards the cashier's counter, painfully aware of the shotgun lying only a few feet away from her. If she was quick she could get it and be out of the door before the stiff even knew she was there. Should she risk it? A gun could mean the difference between life and death. 250 miles left to Orlando. Who knew what would be waiting on the road.

She jumped up and snuck over to the expired shop keep without making a sound. It took her a few seconds to wrench the gun from his stiff cold fingers. She was just about to poke her head from behind the counter when she heard the sound of sugar and macaroni crunching under heavy feet. Her body went numb. The stiff was *much* closer than she had anticipated. She heard the door creak again.

Shit! she mouthed.

There were at least two of them now, maybe more. Why didn't she secure the door when she spotted it earlier? Lt. Harry Wilson would shit his pants if he could see her now.

She clutched the gun to her chest. It was loaded, but she wouldn't risk firing it in here unless she had absolutely no other choice.

If you think breakin' some glass or bangin' a door shut draws them in, just imagine what gunfire does. Easiest way to get yourself killed. Reserve gunfire for the most critical of situations, Mackey. Don't you fire that thing unless you're sure that 1) you can get the hell out of there once you've pulled the trigger, and 2) whatever you're shootin' at isn't gonna get up again.

Mac wasn't sure of either of those.

Her brain was working rapidly. She'd have to see what was happening on the other side of the counter before she could fully assess the situation. She was going to have to risk a glance around the corner. But she didn't have to. Just as she was about to move into a kneeling position, something rounded the bend at the far end of the store, coming up the aisle directly next to the counter. There was nowhere she could hide.

The stiff shuffling along the aisle had been a teenager when he got bit. He was wearing a red apron with the words *Stop 'n Go* printed in cheerful white letters on the front. Half of his face was missing, and his teeth were clearly visible through the hole in his cheek. His eyes were two milky white globes in a mess of rotting black flesh. With each labored step chunks of skin swayed rhythmically from his jawbone on the side of his face which had evidently been eaten off by his killer. It seemed to Mac like an entire lifetime had passed by the time his dead seeing-but-unseeing eyes spotted her. He snapped out of his docile state and barreled down the aisle towards her, his teeth snapping against each other so hard she could hear them cracking.

She had no choice but to jump up and over the counter. She felt his fingers get caught in her hair just as her feet touched the ground. With a painful yank of her head she tore free from his grasp, probably leaving a bit of her scalp behind. The other stiff came at her from another aisle, but she was quicker than its outstretched arms. In one swift movement, she grabbed her backpack from the floor and pushed through the door, her hands around the gun in an iron grip.

She sprinted down the street. The commotion in the store was bound to attract others, she had to get out of the area, and fast.

She rounded a corner and nearly dropped the gun. There was a whole horde of them shuffling aimlessly down the street. Cars were parked on either side of the road, creating an undead funnel straight towards her. No wonder she hadn't seen any that morning – they were all congregating in one bloody spot. They noticed her almost immediately, and before she could so much as catch her breath, an entire crowd of them came running at her down the road. She backed up into the street she'd come from, only dimly aware of another stiff in a red apron coming at her from the direction of the Stop 'n Go.

She ran.

Put as much distance between you and them as possible. One stiff attracts another. If they can see you, they're gonna chase you.

Mac sifted through every bit of advice Lt. Harry Wilson had ever given her, but came up short. All she could do was run. Her brain was preoccupied with the sole purpose of getting the hell out of there.

She had put quite some distance between herself and the horde when powerful hands grabbed her from below. Excruciating pain shot through her arm as a pair of yellow decayed teeth sank into her wrist. The shotgun clattered onto the tarmac as she pressed the palm of her free hand onto the rotting face of her attacker. She could feel the skin and flesh move under her hand against the stiff's skull as she shoved his head back. The lower half of his body was gone. His torso had been lying in wait in front of the car as she ran past. Her arm came free of his teeth, but only after he had managed to take a giant chunk of it. She stepped back, looking down at her arm in horror. Blood gushed from the wound onto the ground. She was in shock. The dead thing was clawing its way across the road to her, his teeth clattering together. With revulsion she saw bits of her own flesh lodged between its teeth.

For the second time that day unseen hands grabbed her, this time from behind. But this stiff had somehow retained the ability to speak, cos it was saying something to her.

"Move!" it shouted.

She turned her head. What a peculiar stiff this was. His eyes weren't all milky and messed up either.

"We have to move!" it said again, grabbing her by the shoulder.

She snapped out of her daze and nodded. She followed him through a maze of side streets and alleyways until he burst through a fire door on the side of a large office space. Once inside he barred the door with a heavy desk and turned to look at her. He was young, probably the age of apron-boy, but his face was lined and grim like he'd seen the end of the world. Mac wondered what her face looked like.

"Sit down," he said, motioning to a leather swivel chair next to another desk. She sat. She seemed to have lost the ability to speak or to make her own decisions. Yup, she was definitely in shock. The pain in her arm was throbbing violently, blackening the edge of her vision.

"I'm sorry," he said as he stood in front of her, "but we have to do this quickly."

In one sudden movement, he raised a machete above his head. Mac only had a brief moment to see it glint in the ray of sunlight shining through the window before it landed on the desk next to her with a dull thud. She looked down at it, surprised at the widening pool of blood forming on the polished surface. It was only after she saw her own severed hand twitching on the other side of the blade that the darkness overtook her completely and she passed out.

...

"Mac, get out of here!" her dad shouted.

He was leaning against the door, holding the crowd of undead on the other side of it at bay.

"Dad, I'm not leaving you!" she screamed back.

"Mac, listen to me!" sweat was running down his forehead into his eyes as he strained against the door, the horrible sound of fingernails against wood chilling her to her very core, "you have to go. Take my bag. The map is there, everything is there. Go to Orlando."

"Dad, we can make it!"

"Mac!" the door opened slightly, but he managed to bang it shut again, "Please, baby, you have to go. I can't hold them for much longer. You can climb out the window, there's a fire escape."

Mac looked to where he dad was motioning with his head, but she couldn't do it. She couldn't leave him. If he was going to stay, then so was she. They would die together.

"Mac," he said as if reading her mind, "No. You have to go. You have to stay alive!"

"Daddy," she cried, "I can't do it without you."

"Yes you can, baby," tears were rolling down his cheeks, *"You're so strong! Remember what I've told you, Mackey. Now go!"*

"Dad!" giant sobs were wracking her body.

"I love you, Mackey."

"I love you too, daddy."

Mac jerked awake, a scream lodged in her throat.

"It's okay," someone said from next to her, "You're okay."

The room was dark except for a single burning candle. Mac was lying on a pile of blankets, her body drenched in sweat and shivering. She looked up into the face of the guy who had saved her. The guy who had cut off her hand.

"You must be hungry," he said, walking over to the candle. The smell of cooking food made her stomach rumble shamelessly and loudly.

"Does that answer your question?" she asked in a hoarse voice.

He smiled at her over his shoulder. She could feel the weight of her arms next to her body, but she refused to look down at the one the stiff had sunk his teeth into. She couldn't bear to see a stump right now. Not yet. She was mercifully free of any pain whatsoever.

"I hope you don't mind," he said as he lifted an empty can of Campbell's Chunky New England clam chowder, "I staked out that store for two days before you came down on it in one fell swoop."

He chuckled as he dished some of the chowder into a coffee mug missing a handle.

"Sorry about that," she croaked.

"Don't be," he replied kindly, "We all have to take care of ourselves the best we can now. What with the world going to shit and all."

He placed the mug on a wooden tray and carried it over to her. With some maneuvering, he helped her to prop herself up against the wall and put the tray on her lap. Instinctively she reached for the tray with her left hand but found that there were no fingers to move. The end of her arm, where her hand used to be, was covered in thick white bandages. She could only stare at it for a while.

"You'll get used to it," he said as he sat cross-legged next to her.

"Are you a doctor or something?" she asked as she spooned some chowder into her mouth.

"Med student," he replied with a shrug.

They finished their meal in silence. Mac couldn't bring herself to consider the implications of traveling across the state with half of the hands she had yesterday. Orlando seemed further away than it had when she was on the other side of the country.

"What's your name?" he asked as he cleared away their dishes.

"Mac," she said, smiling weakly.

"I'm Kyle," he said, sticking out his hand but retrieving it almost immediately, looking embarrassed.

"Why doesn't it hurt?" she asked, lifting up her stump.

"Ah, that would be the super strong painkillers," he replied, "Being a med student gives you the advantage of knowing the good stuff from the *really* good stuff."

She chuckled, hoping he had a lot more where that came from.

"Is Mac short for something?" Kyle asked, the candlelight flickering across his face.

"Makayla," she replied, "but no one ever really calls me that."

"Where you headed?" he asked, lying down on his own pile of blankets and folding his arms behind his head.

"Orlando," she said with a sigh, "My grandparents are there."

"I heard it's safe there," he said, glancing at her.

"Yeah, it is," she moved down onto her back again, feeling extremely sleepy, "My dad and I, we've been traveling from San Francisco."

Kyle made a whistling sound through his teeth.

"That's a long way to go," he said.

"We've... I've made it this far."

She looked up at the ceiling and the intricate shadows the flickering candlelight created there. Lt. Harry Wilson was silent, muted by the drugs.

"You should get some sleep," Kyle said, getting up and moving towards the candle, "You've lost a lot of blood, but you're okay, the infection didn't get a chance to spread. We would have known by now if it had."

"Kyle," she said before closing her eyes and drifting off into a blessedly dream-free sleep, "Thank you."

...

"How much further?" Mac asked for the hundredth time that day.

"About ninety miles," Kyle replied patiently from the driver's seat.

She liked him. There were times when he reminded her of Lt. Harry Wilson, and that made her smile. They were only ninety miles from Orlando, and Mac was getting restless. Their last few days of traveling had seen insane amounts of rainfall. She wondered if the rain had any effect on the stiffs whatsoever, or if it just softened them up some more like overripe tomatoes baking in the sun.

The world is gonna be a green place after this, Mackey, what with all the fertilizer walkin' around.

"Shit, Mac," Kyle said from next to her, easing on the break of the Lexus they had lifted from a liquor store's parking lot. Some drunk had left the keys in the ignition, or that was at least the story Mac told herself.

The road was blocked by a camper lying on its side. Stiffs were ambling along around it like religious zealots around some kind of holy relic.

"We have to go around," Mac said almost automatically.

Protect the vehicle at all costs, Mackey. If it looks like trouble, go 'round if you can. Don't stop. There are things even worse than stiffs, unfortunately. But check the terrain before you do anythin' or you'll get your ass stuck in a marsh or your tires blown to hell or somethin' equally unpleasant.

"Wait," she said as Kyle started moving onto the dirt next to the road, "something doesn't feel right. Go back."

"Mac..." he started, but she interrupted him.

"Just trust me! Go back," she scanned the surrounding trees but saw nothing out of the ordinary - if you count walking corpses as ordinary, of course.

"Something about the camper wasn't right," she said as they drove back the way they came to yet another back road leading out of there, "I wonder how it got that way."

"Who knows," Kyle said, exasperated, "Maybe a bee flew in the window and stung the driver on his fucking eyeball."

Mac laughed, but Kyle didn't. This was the umpteenth time they had to turn around and go back the way they came to try another road. Their options were declining radically.

"I just didn't trust it," Mac said softly.

"Lt. Harry Wilson?" Kyle asked.

"Lt. Harry Wilson," she sighed.

Their humble abode for the evening was an abandoned farmhouse which looked to Mac like something out of The Amityville Horror, a movie she watched without her dad's knowledge and against his wishes. It was something which still gave her nightmares, though she would never admit it.

The sky was a dark and violent gray, the smell of an approaching storm in the air. They didn't have any food left, so their stomachs provided the background noise during the brief interludes of thunder silence.

They were only about 50 miles from Orlando, but they couldn't risk driving through the storm. They'd come this far, and to end it all now in some muddy car accident would have been the most rotten cherry on a cake of flesh.

Mac was telling Kyle about the book of wisdom she wanted to compile when a deep voice spoke behind them.

"Hands," it said, after which there was the distinct sound of a shotgun being cocked.

This must be some cosmic joke, Mac thought as she lifted her stump into the air.

"What have we got here, Roy?" another voice said.

"Two young lovers enjoying the end of the world," Roy responded.

Heavy footsteps creaked on the wooden floorboards.

"We don't want any trouble," Kyle said, casting a quick glance at Mac.

There may come a time when people are a greater threat than the undead. Be still, Mackey. Do what they want, and don't provoke them. Stay alive. But you keep your eyes open. Wait for them to reveal the weakness they inevitably have. Bid your time, and run.

"We don't want no trouble neither," deep voice said, "but we *do* want the keys to the car."

"Please," Mac found her voice, "we're going to Orlando. It's safe there. You can come with us."

Deep voice laughed.

"Hear that, Jamie? It's safe in Orlando."

Jamie made a noise which Mac could only associate with a pig rolling in shit. She cringed on the inside. The laughter died down and was followed by an intensely uncomfortable silence. Mac wished she could turn around and stare her assailants in the face. She hated feeling like a coward. Lt. Harry Wilson wouldn't have been a coward.

"Keys," deep voice said, "or we'll take them off your corpses."

"They're in my pocket," Kyle said nervously.

"Jamie, get."

More footsteps.

"Nice and easy now young pup," Jamie said as he fished the keys out of Kyle's pocket.

"Here's what's gonna happen," deep voice said authoritatively, "we're gonna go out the front door and close it nice and tight, do you folks a favor by not lettin' in the dead ones millin' about on the porch, and we're gonna drive on outta here without any trouble. Got it?"

Mac and Kyle nodded in unison.

"Roy," Jamie moaned, "the girl."

"Jamie, she's not..."

"You promised!"

"Okay, okay!"

The floorboards creaked again. Mac could feel the heat coming off the man standing behind her. She felt cold steel against her skin as he pressed the barrel of the gun against her neck.

"You're comin' with us," deep voice said.

"No, please," Kyle said, getting ready to stand up.

"Sit down!" Roy roared, chilling Mac's blood. She could tell he wouldn't think twice of shooting Kyle right in his face.

"You," he said, pushing the gun deeper into her neck, "Up. Now. Or we feed your boyfriend to our friends outside."

Mac got onto shaky legs, tears threatening in her eyes.

Don't be afraid, Mackey.

She turned around and faced one of the biggest men she had ever seen. His long black hair was tied back in a greasy ponytail. She gauged that four of her could fit inside one of him. Jamie was standing in the doorway, the opposite of Roy in appearance, but she thought she could bet her life on them being equally rotten on the inside.

"Let's go," he motioned to the door with his gun.

"Mac!" Kyle shouted as she reached the door, "I'm... sorry."

"It's not your fault," she managed before being huddled out of the house.

Roy and Jamie's *friends* came at them as soon as they stepped onto the porch, but their sluggish dead limbs were no match for her captors' guns. Their faces were smashed in as soon as they were within reaching distance. Mac looked back at the house as she was ushered into the back seat of the Lexus. Roy and Jamie had lied. They'd left the front door wide open. Mac screamed in horror as she saw two stiffs wander through the entrance, hoping Kyle could hear her.

Tears were streaming down her face as the farmhouse disappeared behind the trees.

"Quiet down, now," Roy said from the driver's seat.

"What do you want?!" Mac screamed at them.

Roy stepped on the break, causing Mac's face to smash into the seat in front of her.

"I said, quiet down!" Roy snapped, "Keep your mouth shut or I swear to Christ I will break your teeth."

Mac's lip trembled, but she held her tongue. Lt. Harry Wilson would do as they say until he could escape. Mac had never missed her dad more.

The sun was hanging low on the horizon, casting its orange light onto the dark clouds above them in beautiful shades of pink and purple. Mac hadn't stopped to appreciate the beauty of the world for quite some time, so she allowed her eyes to drink in all the magnificent colors of the sky. She had the nagging feeling that she wouldn't have the opportunity to do it again for a good long while.

"What's this?" Jamie asked, waking Mac from her thoughts.

They'd reach the same camper she and Kyle had come across earlier that day.

"We go 'round," Roy said simply.

He moved the Lexus onto the dirt next to the road, overtaking the camper at a dangerous speed. There was a deafening pop as the car swerved and slid over the dry mud. Roy cursed as he tried to straighten out the steering wheel, but the wheels had locked. Everything was moving in slow motion then. Mac saw the world outside of the car spin around and around until everything tipped and tumbled. Her head smashed first into the ceiling, and then into the window, then into the ceiling again.

It was a while before she realized that the car had come to a stop. The silence was deafening. Mac lay on the ceiling of the car, trying not to move anything.

Assess your injuries before trying to get out, Mackey.

Her ears were ringing and her head hurt something fierce, but Mac managed to move both her legs and arms. She turned her head to where Roy and Jamie had been, but they must have been flung through the windscreen because she was alone in the wreck.

Blessedly, her ears stopped ringing, and she could hear the wheels of the car still spinning aimlessly above her. There was also a sharp hissing sound she didn't recognize, probably some part of the engine destroyed in the roll. She heard another sound which made her stomach sink - the gurgled, throaty gagging of the dead. The missing windscreen was the easiest way out. Mac crawled over the broken glass, struggling with only one hand. Sharp shards cut at her knees and palm, but she pushed through. Her head was swimming by the time she finally escaped the car. Darkness threatened her vision, but she took a deep breath, refusing to pass out.

Bits of debris were lying on the ground around her. Her eyes searched the wreckage for Roy and Jamie, and when they finally found them she couldn't help but feel pity for the sons of bitches. They were lying a few feet from each other, arms outstretched like they had been reaching for one another in their final moments. Bent over them were half a dozen ghastly forms, each one in different states of decay. Her captors' intestines were spilled onto the dirt as the dead feasted on them.

Mac saw her opportunity and slipped behind the camper out of sight. She had two options – she could run in the direction of Orlando (so close she could almost taste it), or she could follow the road back to the farmhouse, back to Kyle. It was an easy decision.

The fact that she had escaped the crash with but a bump on the head was nothing short of a miracle, and the weight of the situation wasn't lost on Mac as she jogged down the road. The sun had almost set completely, and with it came the chill of the night. Thunder roared in the sky above, and a small drizzle began to fall. Mac pushed forward, her lungs burning. Every now and then she had to catch her breath and stop the dizziness from overtaking her. All she could think of was Kyle, and finding him alive and okay at the farmhouse.

Family, Mackey, is more important than anything. In this world, now, you have to find your own family. A family of strangers. But keep 'em close, like I keep you close.

Kyle was her family now. He was the only thing she had in the world now, and she would do anything to get back to him.

It felt like hours later when she finally spotted the farmhouse in the dim light reflected from the storm clouds above. It was raining, but not heavily. The wind had picked up, whipping the tree branches violently from side to side. Mac ran up the stairs to the front door, which was closed. She managed a relieved smile as she caught her breath and reached for the knob.

"Kyle!" she shouted as she entered the house, "Oh my god, I thought you were dead. I saw.."

The words caught in her throat. Kyle was standing in the doorway leading to the living room where earlier that day they had sat and laughed together. His face was sunken and pale, his skin drenched in an unhealthy sweat. A gaping wound on his shoulder was leaking blood onto his shirt and down his arm.

"Mac," he said, smiling weakly, "I didn't think I would ever see you again."

The words seem to take the last bit of his strength. His legs collapsed under him and he fell hard onto the floorboards. Mac ran to him. The wound on his shoulder smelled foul, like he was already starting to rot even though his heart was still beating.

"I got 'em, Mac," he said wheezily, "I killed the stiffs."

Mac laughed through the tears. Just a few days ago he had told her how barbaric a term that was.

"You're gonna be okay," she said with a sob, "You're okay."

But Kyle hadn't heard her. His eyes were staring past her, and his breathing had stopped. He was dead.

Mac put her head on his chest and screamed. Her only family taken away. Again. She was alone. Again. The world was a horrible stinking place, and she hated it.

She left the farmhouse in a daze, just as the storm hit properly. She wandered down the road aimlessly, unaware of the rain slamming against her body. She didn't fight when a figure came at her from amidst the trees. She didn't scream as rotting teeth sank into her skin.

...

A horde of the living dead wandered down the road to the heavily guarded roadblock just outside of Orlando. Soldiers sat in the sun on the wall, sweating in their weighty gear. The horde gurgled and groaned, but had nowhere to go. Among them was a young girl with one hand, cherry red Doc Martens shuffling in the dust.

CEMETERY THINGS by Jennifer Benn

Katie was sitting on the floor of her dorm room. Papers and books were strewn around her in an arc. So far, her junior year of college had consisted of nothing but all-nighters, energy drinks, and stress eating. Her roommate's television was blaring something about a revolutionary treatment for brain tumors. "Mia, could you turn that down please?" The racket made it hard to focus. She had already read the same sentence three times.

"Mia!" Katie yelled in frustration over the news anchors as she slammed down her chemistry book. The book's hardcover sounded like a gunshot as it struck the floor. Katie tugged her black t-shirt down as she stood up. She hooked her fingers into her belt loops and jumped a little as she wiggled her jeans higher on her hips. She stomped across the living room to Mia's bedroom. Her eyes bulged in annoyance as she glared from the doorway.

Mia had her toothbrush hanging out of her mouth. A slight, minty froth gathered at the corners of her lips. Damp hair clung to her shoulders from the shower, and the steam still lingered in the air. Mia was sitting on the edge of her bed. Her blue comforter and wet towel were in a heap on the floor. Mia's eyes were wide as she kept watching the screen. Light from the television played across her face as the scenes shifted. Katie walked over to her with an exasperated sigh and plopped down next her. The TV was looping footage of a brain cancer patient who had been undergoing the newest treatment. They called it Recusant. It was an injection that targeted the mutated tumor cells and shrank the cancer. Katie watched as the video clip showed a man whose skin was sallow and cheeks were sunken in. Her frustration melted into horror as she watched, both repulsed and fascinated at the same time. She couldn't make herself look away. The patient looked more skeleton than a man. His eyes were wide and crazed as they darted back and forth hardly blinking. The tendons in his neck threatened to snap and burst free as he strained against his hospital bed. The orderlies were trying to secure his restraints, but the man lashed out at them. A nurse ran in to help hold him down, and the man sunk his teeth into her forearm. The footage cut off abruptly and looped back to the beginning. The pane zoomed out to show the reporter in the studio while the hospital footage continued in the top, right-hand corner.

"Nurse Lee is still in critical condition and has begun to show signs of brain damage in her prefrontal cortex. Doctors caring for the injured nurse say that this area of the brain is responsible for behavior and personality. At this time, her cortex is being monitored by regularly scheduled MRI's, but specialists say there is a steady decrease in its size. Nurse Lee and the other patients who have undergone Recusant treatments are being closely monitored." The news anchor's voice remained emotionless through the story as she transitioned nonchalantly to the weather segment.

Mia turned slowly towards Katie. Her eyes welled up, and she pulled the dangling toothbrush out of her mouth with a shaking hand. Mia's mom had been one of the first patients in the trial study for the 'revolutionary scientific breakthrough of the century.' At first, it had been going well. There were improvements. There was even hope for a full recovery, but as the doses increased, the side effects became more apparent. Now, Mia had just seen a sneak peek at what was going to happen to her mother. Katie's heart sagged as she hugged Mia tightly through her sobs.

Katie's phone started ringing in her pocket. She pulled it out and saw Kacey's face on the screen. She hadn't kept in touch very well with her little sister since school had started back up. Guilt settled in the pit of her stomach. Kacey was in high school now. She played the flute in the marching band and was on the debate team. She had texted Katie a few times this semester and asked if she could make it to her recital or come watch her debate, but Kacey had been so overwhelmed with her classes that she had never even texted back. The guilt twisted in Katie's gut as she slid her finger over to ignore the call from her little sister. She focused on rocking Mia gently. The rhythmic swaying helped to calm them both. Katie could feel warm tears seep into the shoulder of her t-shirt. Her roommate's muffled cries were punctuated with sharp inhales as Mia's body tried desperately to remind her to breathe. Katie's phone rang again. "I've gotta take this." Katie's voice was gentle and comforting, but the guilt squirmed in her stomach, "I'll be right back, ok?" She gave her roommate an extra tight squeeze and handed her the teddy bear that was laying on Mia's pillow. Mia curled up on her bed and squeezed the bear to her chest, still rocking slightly. She reached out and took the picture frame from her bedside table and ran her finger over her mom's face. The glass had a light sheen of moisture from remaining humidity in the room. Her fingertip caused the glass to squeak as it skidded along the surface. The picture was from Mia's high school graduation. She and her mother had the same dark hair and the same slender build. People had always teased them that they could be sisters, but that was before the cancer had taken hold.

"Hello," Katie half whispered into her phone, "Kace, this isn't really a good—what? Wait. Slow down. Who's doing what now?"

Kacey's voice was panicked, "Some of the patients escaped! CDC has put up roadblocks and the town is under quarantine. They're attacking people! The news said they've already had two confirmed murders, and at least five are injured. Mom's out of town on business, and dad isn't answering his phone. I'm scared, Katie. I dunno what to do." Katie could hear her sister begin to hyperventilate.

"Whoa, hold on." Katie was trying to process all of this at once. People like that guy on TV were out roaming the streets, killing people, and Kacey was home alone. "Ok," she said trying to kick herself into adult mode, "lock the door. I'll be there as soon as I can. Don't let anyone in. Promise me."

"I...I promise." Kacey's voice faltered between her quick, shallow breaths.

"I mean it, Kace. No one." Katie hung up the phone. Her thoughts were racing. She had been a crappy sister the past few months, but this was more important than her studies. When it really counted, she had to be there for Kacey. The guilt in her stomach writhed and solidified into a formidable foundation of determination. Katie let out a slow, deep breath as she allowed the situation to sink in.

"Hey, Mia," Katie walked gently back to Mia's doorway trying to remain calm for her friend's sake, "I gotta go. Kacey needs me right now...are you going to be ok? Do you want me to call someone for you? Jack, maybe?" Mia's boyfriend wasn't the best at emotional support, but at least it was something. Katie's heart thudded and drummed against her ribs, but her external, placid façade remained in place.

Mia sat up still clutching her ragged, tear-stained bear, "Would it be ok if I just came with you?" Her voice was meek, and she looked so vulnerable.

Katie looked at her and weighed the options. This could be dangerous, and Mia wasn't in the right frame of mind to deal with that right now. She wasn't in the right frame of mind to be left alone either, though. If Katie left Mia behind, she would be worried about her and wouldn't be able to focus fully on taking care of Kacey. There was a rumble outside and the sound of screeching brakes. "What the hell?" Kacey strode over to the window. Military jeeps had started to form a perimeter around the campus. "Shit. Mia, grab your crap. We have to go."

"What is it?" Mia walked up to the window and saw the insignia on one of the vehicles. "Why is the National Guard here?"

Katie grabbed her backpack and dumped its contents on the floor. "Some of the Recusant patients escaped the hospital," she said while shoving an extra hoodie and a couple bottles of water into her bag. "Kace said they were putting up quarantines. Mom is out on business, and she can't get ahold of dad." Katie paused, "Do we have any weapons?" It was such a weird question to hear herself asking.

"Weapons?" Mia looked at Katie quizzically. "We have steak knives, but that's about it. Did...did she say which patients?" Mia had followed Katie into the kitchen. "Why do you need a weapon?" Mia's second question was an afterthought. Her mind was focused almost entirely on one uncertainty: Was her mother one of the escapees?

Katie stopped rifling through the silverware drawer and looked up at her friend. Mia was pale as she clutched the edge of the counter. "No," Katie's voice was empathetic, "she didn't say any names, but some of them have already hurt people. I just want to be prepared. Get together some clothes and anything else you want, ok? We have to leave before they get us all blocked in. We can call the hospital when we get to my parents' house and check on your mom."

Mia nodded meekly and went to her room to pack her things. Her arms stayed still at her side as she walked, trancelike, into her bedroom. Katie went back to looking through the kitchen drawers. Spoon, spoon, fork. "Where the heck are all of our frigging knives?" She mumbled to herself. She opened the dishwasher which was packed full of dirty dishes. The smell of caked on food busted free from the opening. "You've got to be kidding me." Katie wrinkled her nose, pulled out two of the cleanest looking knives in the silverware section, and started scrubbing them in the sink.

"Remain calm. Everyone stay in your dorms." A voice echoed from a speaker outside.

"Let's go, Mia!" Katie yelled from the kitchen while she wiped the knives off on a dish rag. She slung her backpack over her shoulders and grabbed a ball cap to cover her short, messy hair. Mia came out of her room with a duffle bag strap swung across her body. Her wet hair was tied up in a ponytail. Her green shirt was darker where her hair had dripped on it, and the hems of her blue jeans were frayed. Katie handed her a knife.

"You really think we're going to need these?" Mia held the knife pinched between her middle finger and thumb like it was a dirty diaper she couldn't wait to throw away.

"I would rather have it and not need it than need it and not have it," Katie said matter-of-factly as she opened the dorm door and poked her head out into the hallway. Students were wandering to both exits trying to see what was going on outside. Katie held open the door and let Mia step into the hall before following. She turned and looked around their room before closing and locking the door behind them. The click of the lock had a ring of finality to it. Katie grabbed Mia's shoulders, turning her so that they were looking one another in the eye. "Stay close."

Mia nodded and tried to conceal her panic. The two of them shouldered past their classmates until they reached the glass door that led to the campus grounds. A crowd had already gathered. "I guess no one told the National Guard the best way to get college kids to go somewhere is to either tell them not to go there or offer them free food," Katie said under her breath while she kept an eye on the commotion. There was a soldier placed every two feet across the main entrance to the campus. They kept shifting nervously. Their posture was casual, and even from this far away Katie could tell their boots weren't up to spec. She grew up as a military brat. Her dad was a Marine, and they had lived on military bases most of her life. These weren't combat-tested soldiers, hardened and ready to kill if necessary. These poor guys had barely made it out of basic. They looked like they should be at a frat party, not lined up like a firing squad. Katie tightened her grip on her knife and kept it close to her side as she and Mia walked in the opposite direction from the crowd.

"Miss? Excuse me, miss?" One of the soldiers had spotted them.

"Keep going. Don't look back." Katie grabbed Mia's arm and pulled her along faster. They were almost off the grass. The sidewalk was only a few feet away.

"Miss!" He was approaching them with his gun firmly grasped in both hands. The barrel gleamed in the afternoon sun as he held it upright. Katie could see him out of the corner of her eye. He had dark hair, and his broad shoulders were slumped forward slightly. His long legs were closing the gap. Katie quickened her pace.

Suddenly, an ear-splitting scream cut through the air. The crowd of students started scattering, and gunshots rang out. Katie and Mia instinctively turned towards the sounds and saw three people in St. Mary's hospital gowns near the soldiers. It looked like one of the of the soldiers had tried to talk the patients into backing down, but they had lunged forward and bit him. The guardsmen were now firing at the patients. The bullets didn't seem to faze them. The patients kept chewing on him, and chunks of his flesh made sickening, wet, smacks on the sidewalk as they tore him apart. The soldier who had called out to them earlier looked torn between returning to his ranks or securing the girls. He squared his jaw and locked eyes with Katie.

He sprinted determinedly towards her just as one of the patients grabbed a freshman girl and sank her teeth into the tender flesh of the girl's shoulder. "Let's move!" he yelled at them. His booming voice jolted Katie out of her disbelief at what was happening, and she followed him as he ran past. Mia was still shocked by the massacre that was unfolding in front of the school.

"Mia!" Katie yelled over her shoulder. Mia snapped out of her trance and forced her legs to move.

The three of them ran down Main Street until they were three blocks away from the college. The further into town they got, the more disaster they saw. Bodies were strewn between the stores. Some people were still alive. Thick, sticky blood spurted with every heartbeat from a man who was clutching a gash in his thigh. A pool of blood was forming quickly around him. Those who hadn't been mauled by the Recusant patients were either trying to stem the bleeding of the living or taking this opportunity to loot for personal gain. The chaos brought out the worst in people.

Windows were smashed. Glass and fresh blood gleamed in the sunlight. Men and women fought in the streets for impractical items. A fifty-inch TV wouldn't save them from the epidemic. Liquor wouldn't fend off the attacks. Jewelry wouldn't keep their loved ones safe. They were stupid and materialistic, and they were going to die. Instead of running or securing themselves in a locked building, they were out here stealing. Katie dodged past two men carrying a sofa out of a broken storefront window. Another man ran at her and tried to grab her bag. She swung around and drove a kick into his chest. He sprawled backward looking shocked and then scrambled away. No one and nothing was going to keep her away from her little sister, not this time. Katie looked up to see the soldier looking at her surprised and slightly amused. "What?" She asked defensively.

"No, nothing. Just surprised you landed that kick is all." He said with a smirk. "Impressive. I'm Eric by the way."

"Mia."

"Katie."

"Where are you guys headed?" Eric kept checking their perimeter. "Do you know anywhere we can ride this out?"

"We're going to my parents' place over on Oak Hill Avenue. My little sister Kacey is home alone right now, and she needs me." Katie hoisted her bag higher on her shoulders and started winding her way through the bodies and the looters. Glass crunched under her sneakers.

Eric let Mia follow after her friend while he took up the rear, "My unit was called in after the police were unable to contain the situation. We were supposed to take the targets into custody. If that failed, the next order was shoot to kill. I never actually thought I would be put in that situation, though." Eric paused for a moment, lost in thought. He had only signed up for the Guard to help pay for his college. In the back of his mind, he always knew it was a possibility that he would see combat, but he never thought it would actually happen. Eric's face hardened as he thought about the decisions he made that had led up to this moment. "You live your life. You go out drinking, and you ignore the people you care about because you're too tired or too drunk to deal with their shit, you know? Then something happens that makes you take a good hard look at yourself." Eric's voice filled with self-loathing, "You know the last thing I said to my mom? I told her I was too busy hanging out with my buds, and I would call her back later. Now I'll probably never get to talk to her again. Not the real her anyway."

Katie glanced over her shoulder at him and saw his name patch. "Lee? Your last name's Lee?" She stopped walking. "Was your mom the nurse?"

Eric nodded. His mouth was a taut, thin line. His Adam's apple quivered, "Every time I close my eyes I see that news footage of her getting bitten. She wasn't even supposed to be there. She took an extra shift to cover for her coworker who wanted to go to her kid's little league game."

"My mom was a trial patient," Mia said quietly. The two of them looked at one another sharing a palpable loss that made Katie's heartache.

"We need to keep moving," Katie said as a woman on the ground started twitching. "We may not have much time."

The three of them watched as their town descended into madness. It was insane to imagine that all of these bodies were your everyday grocers, baristas, and soccer moms. "How could three people cause this much damage?" Katie asked as they passed a minivan that had crashed into a stoplight. The light was flashing red.

"They didn't." Eric was looking straight ahead. His left foot was pointing forward, and his right foot was a pace behind. He slowly lowered his gun from its upright position and aimed it at something moving on the other side of an overturned truck.

Katie backed up slowly until she was standing beside Eric. "What do we do?" She whispered while keeping her eyes on the figure that was still only partially visible.

"See the alley to your left?" Eric's voice was barely audible as he pushed his gun's safety into the off position. There was a light click as it slid into place.

"Yeah." Katie glanced towards the alleyway. Mia was still a few paces in front of them. She was shaking.

"You and Mia go that way. I'll meet you between Spruce and Sycamore Street." Eric had the gun pressed against his shoulder. His finger rested against the outside of the trigger.

Katie placed her hand lightly on Mia's arm. Mia jumped at her touch, and when she turned around silent tears trickled down her face. Katie took Mia's hand and tried to lead her down the deserted alleyway, but she wouldn't move. She just looked back towards the truck.

That's when Katie saw the person move out from behind the bed of the vehicle. She recognized the slender build, even without the dark hair.

"Mom?" Mia's voice broke and she took a step forward. Her knife clattered to the ground. Her mom's head tilted to one side and then slowly rotated to the other. "Mom!" Mia's voice was pained and breathy. She struggled against Katie's restraining hand.

"Mia, no!" Katie grabbed onto Mia's wrist with both hands and dug in her heels.

Mia's mom pulled her lips back to bare her teeth. Dried blood stained her mouth. Her hospital armband glinted in the sun, and her maroon gown fluttered in the breeze.

"Mom...mom, it's me. It's Mia. It's me!" Mia's voice pleaded across the street.

What used to be Mia's mom charged at them. Her bare feet scraped across the pavement with every step. Mia broke free from Katie's grasp and ran towards her mom. Katie fell backward landing on tiny shards of glass that still littered the sidewalk. She watched as her friend raced towards the monster her mother had become.

A single shot rang out across the street. The silence immediately following it was deafening. For a single moment, the chaos around them was completely still. The bullet had gone straight through the skull. Mia's mom staggered in mid stride. She dropped to her knees and then fell, face forward, onto the asphalt.

Mia screamed and dropped to her own knees. She started beating her legs and doubled over letting out the most primal sound Katie had ever heard. Mia began slamming her head into the pavement. The shrill keening escalated in volume as her grief mounted. Katie crawled over to her and pulled her upright. Mia tried to push her away, but Katie held her tight.

"Guys," Eric said, "there's more of them."

His voice brought him to Mia's attention. She elbowed Katie in the chest and scrambled towards him. Her grief doubled her strength. Katie grabbed her ankles, but Mia kicked her off. She got to her feet and rammed her shoulders into Eric's stomach. He staggered backward a few paces before he was able to brace himself against her attack.

"Mia, it wasn't her anymore!" Katie yelled at her. "Stop it! You saw her. That thing wasn't your mom. She had blood on her mouth, Mia. Blood. Those people at the college, the ones who started attacking the students? That is what she had become. She was one of them."

Mia turned from her attack on Eric and looked at Katie. "She was my mom." Mia's eyes were full of sorrow and desperation. She turned to look at her mom's body sprawled in the street. This was the woman who had worked three jobs to help pay for her college, the woman who had put off her chemo treatments because she thought showing up bald at a high school graduation would embarrass her daughter, the woman who had sacrificed so much for her. She didn't deserve this, to be gunned down in the middle of the street because some scientists in a lab created a horrible new drug. This wasn't fair. She had given so much of herself, and now she was just lying there. She looked so frail and helpless. Mia walked towards her mother. She didn't deserve this. That single thought consumed every part of Mia. She didn't deserve this.

There were four more patients emerging from behind vehicles. They were joined by several pedestrians that all had bloodstained clothing and irregular gashes along their arms and upper body. Eric grabbed Katie around the waist and threw her over his shoulder. He headed for the alleyway away from the approaching Recusant patients and their new victims.

"We can't just leave her!" Katie yelled at him.

"She won't come with us willingly, and right now she's more of a liability."

"But she's going to die!"

"And if we stay and try to drag her with us, so will we!" Eric started jogging towards the end of the alley.

From her position over his shoulder, Katie could see Mia kneeling by her mother. She had pulled her mom's head into her lap and was stroking her cheek. They made it around the corner of the building before Mia's screams started. Katie grabbed two fistfuls of the back of Eric's shirt and closed her eyes. After they had gone a few blocks and the screams had faded, Eric set Katie back on her feet. He leaned his gun against the nearest building. He took her face in his hands and rested his forehead on hers. "Look at me." He said. His blue eyes stared into hers. "You can grieve later. I need you to be strong right now. Do what you gotta do, ok?"

Katie stared back at him. She was having trouble breathing.

"Katie, stay with me, ok? Think about your sister. What was your sister's name? Kerry?"

"Kacey."

"Alright, you have to focus for Kacey, ok? Can you do that?" He absent-mindedly stroked her cheek with his thumb and then caught himself.

"Yeah. Yeah, I can do that." Katie steeled herself. She had to think about Kacey. She could deal with everything later. She closed her eyes and took in a deep breath. She could do this. Her eyes flew open. "Where's my knife?" She looked around and then back the way they had come. "I must have dropped it while I was trying to stop—," She couldn't say Mia's name. If she said it, it would be admitting Mia was dead, and she couldn't do that yet.

"Here." Eric pulled a knife out of his combat boot and handed it to her. "Use mine."

"Thanks." The knife was heavier than it looked. The hilt was black and ribbed to fit a man's natural grip. The steel was heavily polished and blinded her momentarily as it caught the sunlight. Katie adjusted her ball cap. "Ahh!" She winced and pulled her hand away. Tiny shards of glass were embedded in her palms from when she fell.

"Let me see." Eric took her hand in his and looked over the area. "We're going to need to get that taken care of. Got any first aid kit stuff at your parents' place?"

"Yeah. We were always clumsy growing up. Mom made sure to keep stuff on hand." For the first time, Katie wondered if her own mother was ok. She's out of town. She'll be fine. Think about Kacey. "We need to get moving." She pulled her hand away from his.

"You said Oak Hill Avenue, right?"

"Yeah. It's just a few streets over, now." Katie repositioned her bag again and started walking in the direction of her childhood home. This neighborhood hadn't been as ransacked as the rest of town. It was almost eerie how untouched everything looked. Cars lined the streets. It looked like at any moment someone would walk out of their house and check the mail or get in their car to go pick up their kids from soccer practice. Eric kept scanning the area. Wind chimes rattled in the breeze. The notes sang out over the deserted streets. Katie walked closer to Eric. He looked at her and smirked.

"What's that?" Katie leaned her head to the right to get a better look at the vehicles that were parked along the street. At the end of the row, there was a group of people with ripped clothing shoving one another. They were tugging on the door handles of a white car. Some of them were beating their palms against the windows leaving bloody handprints behind. Between the rows of shoulders, Katie saw something move inside the car. "There's someone in there." Her eyes grew wide.

Eric looked at the crowd milling around, "There have to be at least ten of them."

"Right. You coming?" Katie tightened her grip on the knife he had loaned her.

"You're insane." Eric looked at her with disbelief and slight admiration. "You got any combat training?"

"I took karate when I was like eight, and my dad taught my sister and me how to shoot when we were growing up."

"So not really. Ok, look, you know those zombie movies where people always say to go for the head? Well, this time, they seem to be right. The brain is affected. If you take out the brain, you take out the threat. Make sense?"

"Zombies. You know, I always thought that if this ever happened in real life I would be better prepared. I'd just grab my zombie survival kit and hole up at Sam's Club. But now here I am, staring at a horde of zombies, about to run in like a crazy person with a knife." Katie turned her head to look at him, "I'm the person I yell at in horror movies."

Eric chuckled, "Or we could go with option B. Your dad taught you how to shoot? You remember well enough?" Katie nodded while he spoke. "You take the gun and cover me. I'll take the knife. All you have to do is not shoot me. Think you can do that?"

"Yeah." The gun felt awkward in her grasp as he took the knife and handed her the rifle.

"You got this. It'll be a piece of cake." He smiled lopsidedly and winked at her. Once his back was to her his bravery melted away. It was all he could do to make his legs move toward the crowd.

As Eric got closer, he could see a small girl in the back seat of the white car. She was frantically trying to stay as far away from all of the windows and doors as she could. Seeing the girl made Eric tap into his last reserves of courage. He took a deep breath and breathed out slowly. He squared his shoulders and readied his knife. He ran to the closest zombie and rammed his knife into the guy's temple. The blade sunk in up to the hilt. He jerked the knife out and drove it into the eye socket of the next one. Behind him, Katie fired the rifle. Her first bullet ricocheted off of the car's left fender. She cussed under her breath and adjusted her aim. Shoot on the exhale. She could hear her father's voice in her head. She fired another round into the shoulder of one of the zombies that were now focused on Eric. Just a little higher. Her third shot went completely through its head. The bullet had enough momentum that it traveled into the skull of the zombie behind the one she had been aiming at. Both of them immediately dropped to the ground. Katie kept firing, and two more zombies fell to the pavement. Eric stabbed and twisted the knife through the back of a woman's head. He placed his foot on the small of her back and kicked her away from him, freeing his weapon. The force of her impact knocked down another zombie. Eric lifted the knife, clutched it in both hands, and plunged it down into the fallen zombie's skull. His lunge brought him down to one knee.

There were only two left. One charged at Eric and tackled him. Eric lost his grip on the hilt of the knife and rolled onto his back, trying to keep the zombie at arm's length. Katie aimed and pulled the trigger. The gun responded with a light clicking sound. She was out of ammo. While Eric was struggling with one of the zombies, the other one was headed towards her. Blood was smeared across its cheek. It looked at her hungrily and smiled gruesomely as it approached. Katie grabbed the gun by the barrel. The metal seared her skin and the heat made her palms itch. She could see Eric fighting to keep a good handle on the zombie that was on top of him as it writhed in his grasp. Spit drooled out of the zombie's mouth and strung down towards Eric's face. As the second one got closer to her, Katie ran forward to meet it and swung the butt of the gun like a bat into its head. The zombie stumbled. Katie kicked him in the gut knocking him to the ground. She placed her foot on his chest and drove the butt of the gun into his skull with all of her strength until bits of brain matter splattered onto the hem of her pants and across the asphalt.

Katie looked up to see the zombie on top of Eric chomping at the air. His teeth were barely missing Eric's cheek. Katie raced over to them and slammed the butt of the gun into the side of the zombie's head. Eric pushed him off and grabbed the knife that was sticking out of the female zombie's skull. He stabbed the last zombie six times before he allowed himself to begin to breathe again. He looked up at Katie who was standing over him. She was shaking.

Eric stood up slowly and wrapped one arm around her. He pulled her into his chest and she let relief wash over her. Out of the corner of her eye she, saw the little girl move in the car. Katie pulled away from Eric and walked over to the blood smeared vehicle. The little girl looked uncertain.

"It's ok. You can come out now." Katie reassured her.

The girl unlocked the door and pushed it open. She stepped out of the car and looked at all of the dead bodies around her.

"Where are you, parents?" Katie squatted down to look the little girl in the eye. The girl looked towards the bushes on the other side of the car. Katie could see an arm sprawled on the lawn. She took the little girl's hand, "You're going to come with us, ok? We'll keep you safe." The little girl nodded.

"What's your name?" Eric asked.

The girl ducked behind Katie. "Gracie," she said timidly. She held onto Katie's pinkie and ring finger.

"I'm Katie, and this is Eric." Katie stood up, "Let's go this way, ok?" The girl nodded as Katie led her away from the massacre. Katie slung the gun over her shoulder as they walked. They heard the rhythmic whirling of helicopters in the distance, but they couldn't see them yet.

"That's it." Katie pointed at a light blue house in the distance. There weren't any lights on. Katie had a sickening feeling in the pit of her stomach. As they got closer, they could see blood smeared across the siding. Katie let go of Gracie's hand. She ran up the worn, creaking porch steps and pounded on the door. "Kace?" She yelled for her sister as she pressed her nose to the window pane. "Kacey?"

Something moved in the shadows of the hallway to the living room. Katie's heart caught in her throat. She backed away as the lock clicked. The door eased open and Kacey looked through the gap at her sister. Katie jerked the door open and grabbed her little sister in a bear hug. She kissed the top of her head and squeezed her tighter while she wiped the tears out of her eyes.

"Come on, we need to get inside." Katie held the door while the others walked into the house.

Eric started pushing the couch up against the closed door once they were all inside. Katie put her back against the arm of the sofa and pushed with her feet until it slid into place as a makeshift barricade. Kacey went into the kitchen, and they could hear the screech of wood on the tile as she shoved the dining room table against the back door.

"Have you heard from mom or dad?" Katie asked her sister while Eric peered out of the blinds into the street.

"Mom called earlier. She said there are roadblocks around the city, and they aren't letting anyone in or out. I still haven't heard from dad."

Katie walked over to the hall closet and shuffled around the extra toilet paper and the q-tips until she found the first aid kit.

"Here, let me do that." Eric took the plastic box from her, and they went to the kitchen sink. Kacey and Gracie sat on the living room floor and turned on the news. From the kitchen, Eric and Katie could hear the news anchors telling people to stay in their homes. Eric turned on the faucet and let the water run over the tips of his fingers while the temperature adjusted. Once the water was cold, he took Katie's hands and guided them under the stream. She winced a little as the water ran over the tiny shards of embedded glass and the shredded, seared skin that was already beginning to pucker. The cool water offered some relief. Eric pulled the glass out of her palms with a pair of tweezers and then applied antiseptic. While he was wrapping her hands in bandages, Gracie came into the kitchen.

"My mommy always said kisses will make you heal faster." She swayed back and forth from her heels to the balls of her feet while she talked.

Eric smirked and looked at Katie. He took her hands and gently brought them to his lips. He maintained eye contact with Katie as he kissed each of her hands. "I think your mommy was right," Eric said to Gracie while he smiled at Katie. Katie blushed and smiled back at him.

"Let's go back in the living room," Katie shook her head and rolled her eyes at Eric. She put her bandaged hand on Gracie's shoulder and guided her back into the living area.

The mantle was covered in Marine Corps memorabilia, tiny porcelain frogs that Katie's mom had been collecting for years, and a few family photos. Kacey was still sitting on the tan carpet on the floor. Gracie snuggled up next to Kacey and put her head in the other girl's lap. Kacey absent-mindedly stroked Gracie's hair.

Katie and Eric sat down beside the other two. The station was showing footage from a news helicopter as it flew over the town. From the air, you could see the piles of bodies that lined the streets and some of the zombies milling around aimlessly. The video footage shrank into the right-hand corner of the screen as the news anchor came back on.

"The government has taken swift action to contain the situation. Everyone is to remain indoors until the affected citizens can be taken into custody. The CDC would like us to remind you that this epidemic does seem to be contagious. If you are exposed to any bodily fluids of an infected person, please separate yourself from friends and loved ones until you can be reached by officials." A S.W.A.T. team had entered the field of vision on the live footage while the reporter spoke. They meticulously cleared each building. A few team members entered each of the premises. Sometimes they came out with civilians. Sometimes they came out alone. A military man joined the news anchor. His chest was laden with medals that glinted under the florescent lighting. Katie never heard what he was saying because someone pounded on the front door. The knocking drowned out the broadcast.

"This is Sergeant Haskell. Is anyone in there?" The man's voice boomed with authority.

"Yes," Katie yelled as she scampered towards the door, "there are four of us!"

"Anyone bit?"

"No, Sir."

"Alright, open the door slowly, and everyone keep your arms in the air."

Katie and Eric pushed the couch out of the way. Eric unbolted the door and slowly turned the knob. The door creaked open.

"Gracie, honey, put your hands up like this, ok?" Katie said as she raised her hands.

Some members of the S.W.A.T. team entered the house cautiously and started checking the other rooms. Team members started patting Katie, Eric, Kacey, and Gracie down.

"Any weapons?"

"There's a knife and an empty rifle in the kitchen." Eric jerked his head towards the other room. The sergeant motioned for two of his men to check it out.

The soldiers who had been looking through the rooms came back. "All clear."

"Alright, let's move these civilians to the med tents and keep moving." Haskell walked out of the door followed by most of his men.

"This way." One of the soldiers pointed his rifle towards the part of town that had already been cleared.

The men escorting them formed a ring around the four of them as they made their way to the edge of town. They approached a yellow hazmat tent. The soldiers watched them enter the tent and then headed back out to rejoin their team.

"Strip, please." A lady covered in a hazmat suit pulled a thin curtain closed between Eric and the girls. She examined each of the girls, methodically checking them for any lacerations. "What happened to your hands?" The lady looked suspiciously at Katie and gestured to someone at the mouth of the tent.

"I fell on some glass, and I burnt myself." Katie grimaced as the woman undid her bandages to get a closer look.

"I'd like to keep you for observation," the woman backed away from Katie, "just to make sure you didn't get any infected fluids in your cuts." A guard came around the edge of the curtain. "You two can put on the green scrubs over there." The lady gestured to a pile of clothes. "You," she looked at Katie, "need to put on the orange ones. Officer Clifton will show you to an observation tent."

"How...how long are you going to watch her?" Kacey was pale and panicked as she slid the green top over her head. She tugged her hair out of the collar and jerked the bottom of her shirt into place.

"The symptoms should be visible in a few hours if she's been infected. If she's still fine by then, she can find you outside of the quarantine."

"And if she's not?" Kacey's voice rose. The woman didn't say anything, she just looked away. Officer Clifton grabbed Katie's upper arm and started leading her away. Kacey clutched at the officer as he tried to escort Katie out of the tent.

"A little help in here?" The woman called out. Eric pushed aside the curtain as another officer came in to subdue Kacey.

"Watch over them, ok?" Katie said over her shoulder. Eric nodded. His breath quickened, but he tried to remain calm on the outside. He adjusted the green scrubs they had given him and took the two girls outside of the tent to where the red cross was handing out food and water to the townspeople who had been cleared.

Katie was taken to another tent with clear dividers and stretchers. The orange scrubs made her feel like a prisoner.

"Lie down, please." Officer Clifton gestured to the closest stretcher.

"Katie?" The man on the other side of the plastic sheet craned his neck to see her.

"Dad!" Katie smiled at him while the officer strapped her to the cold, metal stretcher. The tent smelled like antiseptic. Her dad was covered in a sheen of sweat. "Dad?"

"Too late for me, Katiebug." He smiled, but his eyes were full of sadness. "Where's your sister, your mom, are they..."

"They're fine. Mom was out of town when it happened, and Kacey was already cleared to go in the first tent."

"Baby girl, if you make it out of here, I—," his body seized up as he tried to speak, "I need you to tell your mom and sister that I love them, ok?" His neck tensed up. His breathing was labored. "Tell them I should have been there for more little league games," Katie's dad groaned in pain as he struggled to get the words out, "and parent-teacher conferences."

"Dad they know how—"

"Katie let me finish. I don't have long." The blood drained from his face. "Tell them I'm sorry, ok? I need you to be strong for them when this is over." His eyes started to dart back and forth, unable to focus. "They're going to need you." He convulsed at the end of his sentence.

"Dad?" Katie fought against her restraints. Her legs and arms struggled to find any give in the straps that had her pinned to the stretcher.

"I need a sedative in here!" Officer Clifton yelled to a nurse.

"I love you, Katie" Her dad looked at her as he tried to keep himself from shaking.

"Dad? Dad!" Katie yelled as nurses surrounded her. She moved her head trying to see her father. She felt a needle slide into her arm. "I love you!" She shouted as her mind became hazy. Her eyes closed even though she fought to keep them open. The sedative took hold of her, and the world went black.

After a few hours, Katie came back to consciousness. She blinked and squinted as a nurse shined a tiny flashlight in her pupils. "Do you know your name?"

"It's Katie." Katie pulled her head away from the nurse.

"Good news, Katie. You appear to have no symptoms of the infection. I'm going to take off your restraints, ok? Just lie still."

"What happened to my dad?" Katie turned her head to look at the empty stretcher behind the plastic.

"He was contaminated. We gave him an injection to help him along peacefully." The nurse touched Katie's arm. "He didn't suffer."

Katie tried to fight back the tears as the nurse removed her restraints.

"Please change into these." The nurse handed Katie a pair of green scrubs as she sat up.

Katie felt numb as she changed her clothes. An officer came and showed her the way out of the observation tent. Katie followed, not really paying attention. It was close to twilight now.

"Katie!" Kacey ran to her sister and hugged her. Her mother followed closely behind and put her arms around both of her daughters.

Katie pulled away and looked at them. "Dad...dad didn't make it." Hot tears ran down her face as the words came out of her mouth. Her mother sat down on the ground and placed her head in her hands. Kacey knelt down beside her mom and cried on her shoulder. Katie's shoulders started to heave as she fought the sobs that were trying to finally escape. Behind her, she felt a strong chest against her back. Katie turned around and buried her face into Eric's chest as his arms encircled her. This was the safest she had felt all day. She let her grief wash over her in waves. She thought about Mia and her dad and all of the devastation she had witnessed.

"Where's Gracie?" Katie mumbled into Eric's shirt.

"She found her aunt. She's with her family now." Eric held Katie tighter as she nodded.

"Here, take one and pass it on." A lady handed them a box of candles with a lighter.

Eric and Katie each took a candle. Katie handed the box to her mom. The survivors all stood in silence, mourning their loved ones. Bodies of the infected were being burned in the streets of the town. They could smell the smoke from outside of the quarantine. The flames of their candles flickered and shone out in the dark as the flames from the burning bodies roared in a crackling cackle. The living and the dead were joined, for one last time, in a vigil of flame.

END

DEADVILLE by Tessa Leon

Chapter One

"For today's homework you are to write a 5000 word essay on the female philosopher Hypatia," said Professor Singh to his class of 60, in the large college auditorium.

"Yawn! Is he done yet?" asked Sonya.

"Sssh!" responded Helen. "I need to write this down."

When the class was dismissed, the philosophy students headed outside to the courtyard. It was last class of the day, so everyone hung out, firming up Friday night's plans.

Helen's classmates and best friends hung out near the fountain.

"Is everyone going to the party at Epsilon tonight?" asked Jane.

Mariko and Sonya both responded with resounding yeses. They looked at Helen.

"Nope, not me. I'm room-bound tonight."

"Again?" asked Sonya in her Finnish accent. "You missed last weekend's party too."

"Last weekend was great! I met Juan at the party!" said Mariko in her heavy Japanese accent.

"I haven't met anyone yet, but there's hope right?" said Jane. "Perhaps I should borrow some makeup from Sonya." She pulled out a mirror and had a look at her plain face.

"You look fine Jane," said Helen. "I just need to get this essay done. I have to work at the coffee shop all weekend, and I still need to do my math and my astronomy homework too."

The women all groaned.

"How long is this going to go on?" asked Sonya.

"As long as I need the cash," said Helen. "You guys go and have fun! Tell me all about the party when you get back home tonight. Or, tomorrow morning, ha ha!" She waved them off.

The three ladies headed off to get ready for the party, while Jane headed for her own dorm room. She left the door open and sat at her desk.

She had just started doing some research on her laptop when her friends poked their heads into her room.

"Last chance for fun!" said Mariko.

"Nope, you guys go and have tons of fun! And be careful!" said Helen. "Remember there was that student who went missing last week."

"Party pooper!" said Sonya.

"Bye!" said Jane, with her half-hearted attempt at makeup.

Helen breathed a sigh of relief. Now she could get some work done. Should she close the door? She peered up and down the hallway, but it was quiet. Likely everyone had gone out for dinner, or was already at a party. She'd tackle dinner later. Right now she wanted to outline her essay on Hypatia, Alexandrian philosopher, who'd been brutally murdered by Christians. And to think that they bashed Muslims nowadays. She shook her head.

The Epsilon building was located right next to her dorm. Unfortunately, she could already hear pounding music, so she closed her window.

It wasn't so great being stuck in her room all night. She took a break to eat some leftover pizza from her mini fridge, but then it was back to work. Having to work to pay for college was frustrating at times. Her parents helped, but it simply wasn't enough.

She had just finished her essay, and was going to get started on her math homework, when she heard a piercing scream fill the air.

Chapter Two

Sonya, Jane, and Mariko were squished into the corner of Epsilon's living room. The room was packed with people, with a loud pop song overwhelming most of the conversation.

"I can't hear what you're saying," yelled Mariko.

"Great party!" yelled Sonya back at her.

"Hey, some guy gave me a bunch of lollipops," said Jane.

Mariko pointed at them. "If you suck on that, you'll get high," she said.

"Yep, it's never just candy at a party," said Sonya.

"Oh, but it was safe last weekend," said Jane. "It only gave a nice light buzz. I was completely within my faculties."

"You can say that again. I hadn't realized you were high," said Sonya.

Jane handed them out to everyone. "Here you go. We'll watch out for one another anyway."

"I wonder where Juan is?" asked Mariko. "He said he'd be here."

"It's still early. I'm sure he's on his way," said Sonya.

"Ooh! I hope I'm at the right party! There might be something else happening tonight. I'd better text him," said Mariko, as the song finally died down.

Jane took the wrapper off her lollipop and stuck it in her mouth. Sonya did the same. Mariko was busy with her phone.

"What on earth is that shrieking?"

"I don't know," said Sonya. She pulled the drapes aside and looked out the window. The others at the party were oblivious to anything happening outside. A new CD started playing and drowned out any other sounds.

***

Helen was just heading to the window to see who was shrieking, when a red splat struck it, and its ooze dripped slowly down. She backed off.

"Ahhhh," screamed a voice outside.

Helen peered out the window.

"What on earth?" she asked, her eyes deceiving her. Outside her window Juan, or what had been Juan was reaching up at her window. He had a huge hole in his head, like someone had shot him, but still, he kept on moving. His jaw was spasmodically making chewing movements on what appeared to be a severed hand.

"Oh my god. How I am going to tell Mariko?"

She watched as Professor Singh ran up to Juan and shot him in the head. Finally, his body dropped to the ground.

"How odd," said Helen. "It was almost like he was a zombie."

"Lock your doors and windows," yelled Professor Singh. "Pull the drapes! There are zombies out here!"

Helen waved at him and did as he said. She rushed over and closed her door and locked it. She grabbed her phone and dialed 911. For some reason, it rang busy. She decided to call campus security instead.

"Hello, security? There is some sort of disturbance happening in the courtyard. Oh, you already know? Yes, I'll stay in my room, thanks."

Helen hung up. She didn't know what exactly was happening outside, but she'd better stay safely in here. Perhaps it was another riot, like the one they had in '97.

She just noticed that someone was in her bathroom. They must have snuck in when she had her door open.

Chapter Three

The party was rapidly turning into a drug party. People were becoming more outgoing and social. The noise level of the party had just cranked up a notch, with conversations competing with the fast pop music.

Mariko had given up on trying to track down Juan. She was chatting with guys, while licking her lollipop. Sonya and Jane has long since discarded theirs, and were pouring themselves drinks from the punch bowl. They'd long since forgotten about the noise from outside, attributing it to a drunk college frat boy.

"Oh look," said Jane. "There's that nasty Bev, over there in the corner."

"Ugh, can't stand her!" said Mariko, giving up her chat with the guys.

"That girl is a bully. Even when she pretends to be nice she has an ulterior motive," said Sonya.

"No lollipops for her!" said Jane, and everyone laughed with her.

"Seriously though, she could use one. Look at how uptight she looks over there. Everyone is avoiding her."

"I can't stand people like that," said Jane. "Remember she kept on asking me why I was going to the bathroom during math class? None of her frickin' business."

"Not one social attribute in that one," said Sonya, taking a sip of her drink.

"Come on guys, I didn't come here to talk about Bev," said Mariko. "I'm here to have fun!"

"I don't know about you, but I'm famished! Let's see what's on the buffet table," said Sonya, leading them away from the drinks table and towards the food.

"Now that you mention it, I do have the munchies," said Jane. "Hey look, a deli tray!"

"Check it out, meatballs!" said Sonya.

"Yuck, I hope they have some veggie food here," said Mariko eyeing the table. She found the veggie platter and filled up her plate.

"Hey, I feel a bit nauseous. I don't think that lollipop and the vodka got along. I'm going to the bathroom," said Jane.

"I'll check on you if you're not back in five minutes," said Mariko.

Jane left to use the bathroom out in the hallway.

"No sign of Juan?" asked Sonya.

Mariko shook her head.

"It's okay, we'll meet up later. I'm not his mommy, he can do what he likes," she replied.

"Well, who needs to be saddled down at a party!" said Sonya.

The music was dying down. Again, they heard sounds coming from outside. They headed to the window and pulled open the drapes.

"Cool!" said a voice from behind them.

What appeared to be the figure of student was madly racing around the courtyard. Except it was lit up with fire.

"Holy crap, what's going on out there?" asked Sonya.

"Why doesn't he drop and roll?" asked Mariko.

Surrounding the burning man were several people wielding various types of weapons. The burning man's arms reached out to grab one of them. His jaws were frantically moving, appearing as though he were trying to bite one of them.

The girls heard cries of "zombie!" coming from outside.

"Wow, entertainment!" said a voice from behind them.

Chapter Four

Helen walked towards the bathroom.

"Excuse me? This is a private room. The public washroom is down the hallway," she said to her private visitor.

The girl in the bathroom seemed to just be standing in front of the mirror, looking at her face. She didn't say anything.

Helen decided she had to start getting tough. Students couldn't just barge into her room at any time they wanted. There was a code of entry in the dormers.

Helen walked into her bathroom. She tapped the girl on the shoulder.

"Hello! This is my bathroom," she said.

The girl turned to face her. One of her eyes was missing. Her lips were gone and much of her face was bloodied, like she had been in an accident. There was a terrible stench of decay mixed with the metallic smell of blood. If there were any doubt that she was wearing stage makeup, it was gone when a maggot slipped out of her eye socket.

"Eek!" cried Helen.

The girl turned completely around and started walking towards Helen. She raised her hands up.

"Get away from me you freak!" cried Helen.

***

In the guy's dormer room Jane was using the private handicapped washroom, as there was no ladies' room here. She vomited into the toilet, and felt better. Perhaps she shouldn't mix drugs and alcohol. She rinsed her mouth out and washed her face off.

By now her efforts to cover her face with makeup were gone. But she felt so awful that she didn't care by this point.

Her shoulder was really itchy so she reached inside her blouse to scratch. When she pulled her hand away, it was bloody. Horrified, she pushed her blouse aside. A large flap of skin was hanging down.

She screamed. Was this part of the drug's side effects? To hallucinate? She didn't know what else to do but hunt through the medicine cabinet. She found a first aid kit and cleaned the wound. She sprayed on antiseptic, and then carefully pushed the skin back up. She placed a large bandage on it.

She didn't see anything else wrong, so she decided to head back to the party and tell her friends she was calling it a night.

***

"Holy shit, what is happening?" asked Sonya.

Outside, there were a pack of professors brandishing weapons. Could it be that they were fighting off a pack of zombies? The man on fire was still running around trying to attack people.

The president of Epsilon had turned off the music, and was yelling out instructions.

"Hello everyone! The Faculty wants to inform us that the campus is under zombie attack! This is not a joke! Everyone is requested to return to their dorm rooms ASAP and do not engage with anyone. Thank you for coming to our party. Goodnight."

He then started guiding people out the door.

Sonya and Mariko decided they'd better wait for Jane to come back from the bathroom. They tensed as they saw Bev heading towards them.

"Why do you girls always hang out together?" asked Bev. She was short and had fake blonde hair. She was standing there holding her beer and smirking from behind her Chanel eyeglasses.

"Because we have friends, Bev," Sonya said to her.

"Oh, I have friends too. They invited me to the Vanderbilt party last week, at their big mansion down the street."

"Well, that's awesome," said Mariko, trying not to roll her eyes. "Shouldn't we try to find out what is happening outside?"

"Really?" said Bev. "Because you seem a bit sarcastic to me."

"You started it," said Sonya. "You really need to be more respectful towards people."

"Hey bitch!" started Bev.

"Oh look, Jane's back!" said Mariko. "I think it's time we headed to Juan's party," she suggested.

***

Chapter Five

"Get away from me," cried Helen. The zombie thing came at her.

Helen looked madly around the room for a weapon. What would be in a dorm room that she could use as a weapon? She looked madly around. Books. Pens. Bar fridge. Knapsack. Baseball bat.

That's it, she could use her roommate's baseball bat. The zombie was trying to grab at her arms. Helen picked up the baseball bat and whacked it over the head.

The zombie's head exploded, brains and blood everywhere.

"Ugh," said Helen. "Sarah, is that you?"

She peered more closely at the zombie, and realized that it had been her roommate, who was supposed to be out for the night.

She started crying, but then tried to pull herself together. From what she knew of horror films, the gore on her face could be dangerous. She dropped the bat and rushed to the bathroom to wash up.

Inside the bathroom she stripped off her clothes and headed to the shower. She spent a good twenty minutes ensuring that not a speck of zombie blood remained on her skin. She turned off the water, then used a towel to dry off. Wrapping it around her she carefully picked her clothes off the ground and dropped them in the bin. She then fished bleach, gloves, and a cloth from under the sink, and scrubbed down the floor, as well as the sink and mirror. There was no telling what Sarah had touched as she was turning into a zombie.

She then got dressed. She grabbed her knapsack and carefully opened the door to the hallway. Ten zombies loomed outside. They curiously peered at her as she widened the door. Nope, there was no way she was getting out that way.

As the zombies reached towards her, she hastily shut the door. She was stuck in here, with a dead zombie. Helen grimaced at the mutilated body lying on the ground.

Chapter Six

Jane finished up in the bathroom. She was starting to feel better. In fact, she was downright hungry. She decided to head back to the party, but most likely she would have to call it quits and head to bed.

As she walked backed into Epsilon's living room, she saw Bev hovering over the group. What did she want?

Jane couldn't stand Bev. Bev had taunted her in philosophy class for weeks, until Professor Singh had put an end to it, threatening to call her out for bullying. It was prohibited on campus. Still, it did not stop her from putting in a jab every now and then.

Soon Jane grew to pity Bev, who obviously dealt with bullying from her parents on an ongoing basis. But tonight, enough was enough. Jane was hungry.

Sonya and Mariko waved frantically at her. They watched as Jane strode up and bit Bev in the shoulder.

"Ahh!' screamed Bev. "What the!"

"Oh my god," cried Mariko. "What have you done?"

Jane lifted up her head and licked her lips. "Wow, I don't know what got into me!" she said.

"I'm going to have you arrested for assault!" said Bev, holding her sore shoulder. There was a small amount of blood, but not any more than normal with an animal bite.

"Let's get out of here!" said Sonya. She grabbed her friends' hands and they left the end of the party.

As they hurried out of the building, they saw chaos in the courtyard.

"Damn! What are we going to do?" asked Mariko. "It's a bloodbath out here."

Strangely, as zombies attacked the remaining professors, they avoided their group. They watched as Professor Singh shot a zombie through the head. The zombie went down.

"I think the professor has things under control," said Mariko.

"This way guys," said Jane, and led them around the side of the building. Soon they were safely back in the women's dormitory.

"What's happening?" asked Mariko.

"I think it's the zombie apocalypse," said Sonya.

"Whoa, I thought zombies were only characters in a movie," Mariko replied.

"And what was that biting about?" Sonya asked Jane.

"I don't know what came over me," said Jane. "Am I a zombie?"

Her two friends looked worriedly at her.

"Your eyes seem normal, not like the crazy zombies outside."

"I think I was just angry at Bev, for all this time," said Jane.

"Let's get back to our rooms," said Sonya.

"Let's check on Helen, first," suggested Mariko. She led the way.

***

Inside her room, Helen had tidied up. She'd managed to shove Sarah's zombie body out the window. She'd spent some time mopping up the blood. Fortunately, the flood was linoleum, to making cleaning easier. She'd had to toss out some of her stuffies, but she was an adult anyway, and she had killed a human after all.

Cleaning had calmed her mind somewhat. She was carefully inspecting the floors and walls to be sure that she had left no speck of zombie blood behind. She wrapped up the ends of a large black garbage page, and closed them securely. She could dispose of it once it was safe to leave her room. She still heard moans and groans coming from the hallway, so she was still trapped in her room.

Chapter Seven

Mariko, Sonya, and Jane walked carefully down the hallway. There were some zombies around, but surprisingly, the zombies avoided them. Perhaps zombies only liked older adults? The professors had been fighting them in the courtyard. It was just another mystery of zombie life.

Mariko stopped in front of Helen's door, which was securely shut.

"At least she had the sense to close it," said Sonya.

Mariko knocked on the door. "It's us," she called.

The door slowly opened. Helen's eyes peered out.

"Mariko?" she asked.

"It's just us. It's crazy out there!" said Mariko. "Whoa! It reeks of bleach in here," she said, as Helen opened the door wider to let them into the room. The three women stepped in.

"What's happening out there?" asked Helen. "I had to deal with my zombie roommate! I feel so bad! I had to kill her!"

Mariko and Helen embraced.

"It's not your fault!" said Mariko. "A whole bunch of students have turned into zombies!"

They let go of each other.

"Right guys?" asked Mariko. She turned around.

Sonya was advancing on them. Her eyes glowed a deep red color. Her facial skin was starting to peel away from her face.

"Oh my god! What happened?" cried Mariko.

She and Helen headed to the back of the room. Jane stood near the door looking confused.

"Oh, the bat," said Helen. She looked wildly around the room. Where had she put it during her cleaning?

Sonya raised her arms in the air and advanced towards them.

"Brainnssss," she said. "Must eat brains."

"Is this a joke?" asked Jane, standing there confused.

Helen slipped off to the side to grab the bat. Sonya grabbed onto her wrist.

"Do something!" cried Mariko.

Helen raised the bat and slammed it into Sonya's head. Her head went splat, and her body dropped to the ground.

"Godammit!" cried Helen. "Now I have to clean the friggin' room again!"

"Holy shit! You killed our friend," said Mariko.

"I had to!" yelled Helen. "She was a zombie!"

Mariko started crying. Helen patted her on the shoulder. All this time Jane was cooly watching them from the door.

Helen looked towards Jane.

"Oh no, not you too Jane!"

They watched as Jane's eyes glowed red. Some of her skin was starting to flake off.

"Leave right now Jane! I don't want to have to kill you too!"

"Ohhh I can't watch you kill another of our friends!" said Mariko grimacing.

"I'm not a zombieeeee," said Jane, slurring her words.

"Please leave, while you can," said Helen.

Jane listened and turned away. She left the room. Helen slammed the door after her.

"Holy crap! What just happened?" asked Helen.

Chapter Eight

"We were at a party having fun, when we saw a disturbance outside," began Mariko.

"Yes?" asked Helen. They were both seated on a clean part of her bed, ignoring the gore from Sonya's body around them.

"We saw the professors fighting off zombies in the courtyard. And then they shut down the party. Bev was harassing us, and Jane bit her."

"Jane bit her? And you brought her back here?!" cried Helen.

"Sorry, we didn't know. We just thought she was annoyed." They both looked at each other and started laughing.

After the horrific events of the evening, they both needed a good laugh.

"Well, while you guys were away, I was battling off my zombie roommate."

Mariko looked around the room. "Where is the body?" she asked.

"I pushed it out the window," Helen explained.

"Oh my god. The police are never going to believe this!"

"I know," replied Helen. "We need to do the same with Sonya's body, and then clean up. They'll think they were killed outside."

"Right, let's do it!" said Mariko.

As they were cleaning up, they continued to discuss the evening's events.

"What I don't understand is how the students are suddenly turning into zombies," asked Helen.

"It's strange. Like an infection or something," said Mariko.

"Maybe none of us are immune? We could all turn at any moment," said Helen.

"Very strange. Like there is a common element. It was triggered by something, possibly," her friend replied.

Sonya's brains hadn't made as much of a mess as the last one's. Soon they had the room cleaned up. A second garbage bag now stood by the first.

"We're going to need to dispose of these bags before the police see them in here," said Helen.

"Speaking of which, I haven't heard or seen any around," Mariko said.

"They must have their hands full," said Helen, shrugging.

Mariko was sitting on the bed dead still.

"What's the matter?" Helen asked her.

"I just thought of a common element."

"Yes?" her friend asked.

"When we were at the party they were handing out lollipops," she replied.

"Oh, sugar gets a bad rap, but I doubt it's caused zombiosis."

"No, not that. The lollipops were tainted with some drug, to make us feel happy," said Mariko.

"Didn't we try something like that last weekend? But nothing happened. Why now?"

"I'm not certain," said Mariko. "Oh no!" she cried.

"What's wrong?" asked Helen. "Besides the usual zombies running rampant.

"I had a lollipop too!" Mariko started crying, and put her head down into her hands.

Helen stopped and thought about it.

"If this is a true theory, we'll know for certain when you turn into a zombie!" She grabbed the bat, just in case, but Mariko did not notice. She was too busy crying.

Chapter Nine

Outside Jane was walking around dazed. She saw humans run past her and avoid her. Since she didn't appear to be much of a threat, they left her alone. It had tasted good biting Bev, and she wanted more, but she felt it was wrong to bite humans. Perhaps she could find some deli meat or hot dogs and that would fill her up.

There were several dead bodies, both human, and zombie, in the courtyard. A small gang of professors and campus security were still actively fighting off the more active zombies. Other zombies merely milled around confused, and for the most part were left alone.

Jane briefly wondered if there were different levels of zombies.

***

"Maybe I should leave?" asked Mariko.

"No, please stay. I'm curious as to whether it was the drugs that caused the zombie outbreak. If so, I can get word to the authorities, so at least they can prevent it from happening again."

Helen gripped her bat by her side.

"I wonder what happened to Juan?" asked Mariko. "He never showed at the party."

Helen jumped. "Oh, I'm so sorry."

Mariko raised her head. "Do you know what happened to him?"

"Yes, and it's not good."

Mariko started crying again.

"How did it happen?" she asked.

"I was watching out the window as Juan was trying to get in here. He was a zombie. Professor Singh shot him in the head. I'm so sorry," Helen said, wrapping her arm around Mariko.

"It's okay," Mariko sobbed. "Soon I'll be a zombie too, and you can shoot me in the head."

"No!" said Helen. "We don't know for certain."

***

In the courtyard Jane didn't know what to do with herself. Perhaps she should go back and lock herself in her dorm room? That way she would not be a hindrance to anyone.

"Jane? Is that you?" said a familiar voice. She turned to look at him. Was it her time to die once they realized that she too was a zombie?

***

"Do we just wait here?" asked Mariko.

Helen nodded. "I think it's best. It's safer in here. I've got my bat, I'm armed."

Outside a lot of the noise seemed to be dying down. Helen got up to peer out the window. There were significantly more bodies lying in the courtyard than there had been the last time she looked. So, things were progressing. Until the cavalry arrived there wasn't a lot she could do.

In the distance she thought she saw a woman who looked like Jane. She appeared to be chatting with a guy.

"Say, Mariko, something odd is happening out here," said Helen.

Helen turned to her friend, but she wasn't there. Mariko was at the door trying to move a bookcase in front of it.

"Listen! There's a swarm of zombies out there!"

Mariko was right. Soon there was pounding and banging at the door. The door shook on its frame.

Helen jumped forward to help her friend move the bookcase. She'd take her chances with potentially being stuck in a room with one zombie, rather than the dozen milling outside.

Chapter Ten

Mariko and Helen didn't know what to do. These zombies were smart. They were banging and hammering at the door, trying to get in.

"How do you feel?" Helen asked Mariko.

"Not like a zombie, if that's what you mean," she said.

"Good, so far so good," Helen replied. Though she still clutched the bat in her hands anyway.

The door splintered. The zombies must have been using something to ram it.

"If Jane retained some of her intelligence as a zombie, it stands to reason that these guys have too," said Helen.

"We're going to die," moaned Mariko.

The door splintered inwards, showering splinters and fragments everywhere above the bookcase. The bookcase remained in its place, keeping back the hoard.

Just as suddenly as the door exploded, the zombies were gone.

"Hi guys!" said Jane.

"Jane!" cried Mariko and Helen in unison.

"I've gotten rid of these guys for you now, but I suggest you find a more secure location," Jane said, her words sluggish.

Mariko and Helen hopped over the bookcase and into the hallway.

"This way!" said Jane.

The two women looked hesitantly at each other. Should they trust a zombie? They followed Jane anyway.

Jane led them to Juan's room. Mariko was a bit confused. They walked inside.

"Stay here! I'm helping the professors to round up the zombies outside," said Jane.

She closed the door behind them.

"Oh my god! Juan! You're still alive!" Juan stood by the window. He was indeed well and happy.

Helen was confused. Perhaps she had been mistaken?

"I thought you said he was dead!?" cried Mariko.

Mariko and Juan held each other.

"That was actually my brother!" explained Juan.

Helen looked remorsefully at him.

"I'm so glad your brother was killed and not you!"

Juan let that one go. In fact, Helen had to stifle a giggle. Who could be serious after what everyone had just gone through?

"Oh no! You can't touch me!" said Mariko.

"What?" asked Juan, confused.

"I licked one of the contaminated lollipops. I'm going to turn into a zombie too!"

"Surely it would have happened by now?" reasoned Helen.

"Oh those damn lollipops. You're right, they were what caused the zombiosis." Juan looked concerned. He looked over Mariko's arms, and face, but so far they were clear.

"Tell me Mariko, did you eat a red lollipop, or a green one?"

"What? What difference does that make?"

"Because Professor Singh told me it was the green lollipops that were infected with the zombie drug, not the red ones."

Helen and Juan looked expectantly at her.

"It was... green!" she said.

They all had horrified looks on their faces.

"Ha ha! Fooled you! It was red."

They all burst out laughing.

Someone pounded on the door.

"Yes?" Juan called out.

"Coast is clear," called Jane.

He opened the door. Professor Singh and Jane were standing there.

"It appears campus security has things under control. I recommend you stay here for the night, while we clean up," said Professor Singh. "I'm going to take Jane somewhere safe so we can find a way to cure her, along with some other zombies who helped our cause, rather than killing anyone."

"Bye guys!" called Jane.

"Bye! Take care," her friends called after her.

Juan closed the door. "Who wants pizza?" he asked. "There's always pizza delivery, even during an emergency."

"Me!" cried Helen and Mariko.

"But make mine vegetarian, said Helen and Mariko, at the same time.

"I just had a thought. What happened to Bev?" asked Helen.

Everyone shuddered to think that Bev was now walking around campus as a zombie.

The End.

INFECTIOUS by Robin Romero

"Nam? We are going to Nam?" Chris asked.

Captain Collins gave him an exasperated look. Chris was always the one asking why. It drove Collins crazy.

"Shut up and suit up, Soldier!" he yelled in his best 'don't ask me again' tone.

Chris rolled his eyes and started grabbing his gear. He had served under Collins for three years now and they had an older brother, younger brother relationship. As he pulled on his boots, Chris' best friend and fellow soldier walked into the storage unit.

"Hey Chris, I just heard we are off to Vietnam. Make sure to bring condoms. I heard those girls are freaky." Max said with a smug smile. Chris threw his boot as his friend and laughed. Meanwhile Collins sneaked up behind Max and grabbed his shoulder. Max jumped out of fright and Chris howled in laughter.

"No condoms. No women. Where we are going, there won't be any people." Collins said sternly.

"What?" Max said as he turned to salute his captain. "No people? Where exactly are we going?"

"It's need to know and you two don't need to know until we are landing in the jungle. We leave in two hours." The guys grabbed their things and marched across the hot tarmac. It was summer and the base in Okinawa was scorching. Chris' unit had been training at the navy base in Southern Japan for two years as a special unit. Usually, the army didn't spend much time on Navy bases but for Collins' team they made an exception. As they flew over the blue ocean and watched the islands pass under their feet, Collins debriefed his team.

"Men, this is classified. As in, if you tell anyone, you will die. Now, as you all know, Vietnam and North Korea have been feuding for the past year. Well North Korea has recently sent a threat to nuke Vietnam. President Quan has spent over a billion dollars on research and engineering for a new type of chemical weapon. It is highly localized and sends out a toxin that attacks the lungs and caused them to stop expanding. Being the true humanitarian that he is, he decided to test it on a remote village in the jungle. Unfortunately, there isn't enough proof to hold him on war crimes but we do need to go into the village to clear it as safe and make sure all the dead people are buried or sent to labs for research."

"Wait, he just bombed his own people?" Chris asked in horror. Collins looked at him.

"Yes. And I don't remember telling you it was your job to judge. Now, once we land, you all need to put on your hazard masks and gloves. The chemical is supposed to be dangerous if inhaled but it could also be dangerous if touched." Collins explained.

The plane touched down and the soldiers pulled on their masks. As they walked off the plane and into the tall grass, the heat hit them like a wall. The sun was bright and the humidity was intense. They were sweating immediately. Collins walked in front of them and then stopped. He turned to them to motion that they were going to head into the jungle on a wide path that lead to the now sleeping village.

The jungle was dense but silent and the quiet put them on edge. These soldiers had spent enough time in the jungle to know that there were always noises. But not here. The soldiers walked in to lines, each looking into the forest around them for any signs of animal life. They walked on in silence for an hour until they finally saw the village. Huts were scattered along smaller dirt paths.

A town stuck in time.

Chris, Max and two other soldiers split off from the group and checked each of the huts along the west part of the village. As they approached the first hut, they noticed a white film that covered the ground and outside of the hut. Chris brushed his finger along the wooden door and pull the gloved hand to his face. He brushed the thin powder off on his pants. Max opened the door and the other two drew their guns. The four rushed into the small hut to find it empty. Fresh smoke hovered over a makeshift barbecue pit.

Whoever had been here had left in a hurry.

As they looked around the house, they were hit with the magnitude of the attack on the village. Silently, they checked the rest of the huts only to find the same thing. Houses that looked as if their owners were coming back. They were frozen in that moment. The moment that the chemical had dropped. None of them could shake the uneasy feeling they had in the empty village. They met with the rest of their team in the village center to report in.

"It's like they just left in the middle of everything. Like Roanoke. Wait..." Max said then paused.

Chris picked up his thought. "Has anyone seen any bodies? This stuff is meant to kill them where they stand. Shouldn't there be bodies in the huts? And in the streets?" Chris asked as he looked around.

Collins thought for a moment. "Maybe the Vietnamese army already took the bodies and didn't tell us. I will call this in and see if we are missing some information. First, Miller, check the air and see if we can take off these annoying masks." He barked. A soldier named Miller pulled out a yellow instrument from his back pack and turned it on. It made a few beeping sounds before a little light on the side turned green.

"We are clear." Miller said cautiously. No one wanted to be the first person to test the air. Collins, as always, took the initiative.

"Don't worry ladies, I will make sure you all can breathe. If I die. Go back to the plane and fly back to base. Tell them that the village is still unstable." He said as he undid the strap for his mask. He pulled it off and took in a deep breath. Suddenly, he began to shake violently. He groaned and stumbled to the ground as his team rushed to his side. Then just as suddenly, he stopped, turned and smiled at them. "Got ya!" He yelled.

The soldiers let out a sigh of relief then jokingly punched him for his trick. Then, one by one, they removed their masks and secured them to their back packs. As they looked around and blinked in the sunlight, they wondered where the people had gone. Collins took his phone and walked further away from the group.

"Commander, yes, it's Collins. I need to you check something. I think those idiots in the Vietnamese army are wasting our time. It looks like they already came to clear the bodies. I need you to confirm before we leave." Collins said into the phone. The soldiers couldn't hear the other side of the conversation. They waited as Collins listened intently. Then his face became very perplexed. He glanced at his men then back out to the grass. "Are you sure?... Ok but then... where are they?.... right. Yes sir." And with that he hung up.

The soldiers watched as he walked over to them with a very thoughtful look on his face. "So apparently, no one has come to remove the bodies. It is our job to find them. So, I need theories on where they could be." Collins said.

"Maybe another village took them!" One of the newer soldiers offered and the others laughed.

"What would they want with poisoned corpses?" Collins asked with a snide tone.

"Maybe the North Koreans came and..." Said another one of the Soldiers.

"Ok, Ronald, now I know why you joined the army instead of going to college." Collins said and the men laughed.

"Sir?" Chris started. Collins looked at him and gave him a no nonsense look. "I believe they saw the chemical descend. They felt the effects and maybe they thought they could out run it. I think they went into the jungle to get out of danger." Chris offered. Collins looked at him with an impressed facial expression.

"Good. Lets go with that one. Now we just need to figure out which way." Collins said.

"Oh, sir, I thought I saw footprints in the white dust along the eastern edge of the village. Here, I will show you." Said a soldier by the name of Jack. Collins nodded and the rest followed them to the foot prints.

They were there alright. "Ok, it seems they are heading into the jungle along this path. Does anyone have a map?" Collins asked. Max pulled out his map and found their location.

"Sir, it looks like the closest thing along this path is at least 10 miles away. They wouldn't have made it to another village. I bet they died on the way there." Max said.

"I agree. We will march on this path until we find the bodies. Everyone drink your water now because as soon as we find these bodies, I want them buried or loaded into the plane. Got it?" Collins barked.

"Yes Sir!" They all replied. They each drank from their metal bottles and got into their marching formation. They began walking into the jungle on the new path, following the white powdered foot prints that the villagers had left behind. The noiseless jungle leaving them with only the noise of their own scared thoughts.

The dirt path sloped upwards at a steep incline for about a quarter mile and the soldiers were all silently amazed that choking villagers could have made it up the hill without collapsing and dying. But no bodies were in sight. Once they crested the hill Collins held up his arm to indicate that they should stop.

"Ok men, take a break." He said. While the soldiers slumped over and grabbed for their water bottles, Collins looked at the path ahead and noticed something. He took a few steps forward and saw that there were several small paths that branched out from the one they were on and went deep into the jungle. "Max, give me that map." He said reaching behind him and holding out his hand. Max stepped forward and placed his map in Collins outstretched hand. Collins tore it open and looked at the path they were on. "Strange... none of these paths are marked on this map. Is this map the most updated version, Max?"

Max looked in the corner to see the date it was produced. "Yes Sir, see here in the corner. March 31st 2016. It was made just a few months ago." He explained.

"Shouldn't these maps have a record of every path no matter how small?" Collins asked. Max nodded.

"Maybe they are new paths… Sir." Max offered.

Collins stepped forward and looked at the opening to the first one on the left. "No, look at this. This path has trees growing around it. It's gotta be at least 200 years old." Max stepped forward to look down the trail. Collins walked over to the next path and then the next. There were five the shot off the main road.

"Ok men, we need to check each of these for bodies. I want groups of four to go down each path then report back here in an hour. With this kind of chemical weapon, there is no way they could have walked further." The soldiers nodded and immediately split themselves up. Max and Chris were joined by Collins and Miller. They took the last path on the right. The path was so small that they had to walk single file. Collins was, of course, in front and Max held up the rear. Miller was using his GPS mapper to track their movements so he could add it on to the map later. There wasn't much to see besides trees and bushes. No animals and the only sound was the wind blowing through the trees.

After about 15 minutes they came upon a little creek. The four of them splashed the cool water on their faces and backs of their necks. They were joking with each other and splashing. With such an intense mission, it was always good to blow off steam. Chris was about to send a large splash of water straight into Collins' face when he saw something glistening on the path about ten feet in front of them. Slowly, he walked through the shallow water and over to the area that had caught his eye. As he approached, his smile faded. The glisten was coming from a large pool of syrupy red liquid.

"Captain. You should see this." He yelled over his shoulder as he knelt down to get a better look. Collins looked up at the soldier and made his way over with a long sigh. As he approached Chris, his smile faded too. "I think it's blood, Sir." Chris said. Just then a small breeze wafted the metallic sent up to their noses and they knew for sure it was blood.

"Well, it could be animal blood." Collins said fearing that he was wrong.

"Sir, I haven't seen an animal since we landed." Chris said. He leaned forward toward a bush behind the pool. There was blood on the lower branch. He pushed it aside to see something that would send a chill throughout his overheated body. It was a bloody foot print followed by another and it was headed into the jungle going off the path. Chris looked up at his captain's face. Blood had drained from it. They both stood, looking into the thick jungle in the direction that the foot prints led.

"Let's stick to the path. We will walk another 15 minutes the head back... keep your gun out." Collins ordered. Max and Miller walked up behind them and saw the blood. They pulled out their guns and the four walked silently along the path, keeping their eyes peeled for anything and everything. After another 15 minutes of walking they didn't find anything else. They turned back and walked out to the main path. Their stomached turned when they saw the pool of blood and they walked at a very brisk pace.

Finally they were back on the main road. They all felt a sense of relief and a small sense of safety. They were the first group back but were joined two minutes later by another group of four. They walked up to Collins.

"No bodies sir. It's all clear Sir." One of the soldiers said. He nodded. Chris walked up to Collins and whispered in his ear.

"Sir, shouldn't we tell them about the blood?" He asked. Collins shook his head slightly. Then they waited for the other three groups. The next two came out at roughly the same time shaking their heads.

"No bodies." They all said.

"This is absurd. Where could they be?" Collins muttered to himself. "Maybe group five will have something."

They waited for a half an hour but there was no sign of group five. Collins looked at his watch impatiently. He was annoyed. They were wasting time.

"Did I not say come back in one hour to report in? Where the hell are they?" Collins hollered.

"Maybe they found the bodies and started burying them..." Miller said.

"Does anyone listen to orders in this unit?" Collins yelled again. "Group four, go on that path and find them. When you find them, two of you come back and tell me what they are doing." He ordered. They nodded and walked into the jungle. The rest of them waited, chatting among themselves. An hour passed by. No sign of them. Then finally, they heard running. It was one of the soldiers. He was running fast and collapsed in front of Collins.

"Dave, what are you doing?" Collins asked annoyed that only one of the soldiers had returned when he had told two of them to come back. The soldier laid on the ground in front of him breathing heavy. Finally he looked up and said.

"Sorry sir, I... uh... they're gone." Dave stuttered.

"What do you mean they are gone?" Collins asked exasperated.

"We were walking along the path. I was leading and everyone was quiet. Finally after I had walked a half an hour and I called out for the other group. But I heard nothing. I turned around to see why the other men weren't calling out for the other group and they were gone. Vanished. I looked around and called their names but... no one replied. I walked ahead on the path to see if maybe the other group had gotten further but after ten minutes, I was too freaked out. There was no sign of any of them. I turned back and when I walked along the path I saw a pool of blood and a foot print. Like the kind of foot print that was bare. No shoes so it couldn't have been from one of the guys. I got even more freaked out. I called their names again but... nothing. I started to jog and then I came along another pool of blood and more foot prints leading off into the jungle. It froze my blood. I started running faster. Before I knew it, I had splashed through a third pool of blood but I kept running." Dave said in horror.

The other soldiers shifted their weight uncomfortably. They all looked at Dave then at Collins. Collins was pale but was trying to hide his fear.

"We need to get out of here captain. We will tell them it's not clear." Said a soldier named Ryan. His voice shook as he spoke.

"We can't just leave our men here. We have to find them before we go anywhere." Collins said as he looked at the path way. "Ryan, take Dave back to the village and wait for us there. As soon as we find the others we will head back to the plane." Ryan nodded and helped Dave to his feet. Both shook as they walked back down the large path into the village.

"The rest of you will follow me on this path. We will be singing our army chants the whole way to make sure that no one disappears..." He paused. "Let's go." He said with about as much enthusiasm as a kid going to the dentist.

With a big sigh, Collins took his first step into the jungle. They jogged and chanted for a half an hour. Every five minutes, Collins turned to count his men. He had started this whole trip with 19 men. He was now down to twelve and two of them were back in the village. They past the three pools of blood and tried ignoring the sinking feelings in their stomachs. They ran for 45 minutes and finally Collins allowed them to stop.

"Take a break. We have to go into the jungle. We will fan out but I want everyone to stay within view of each other." Collins said as he looked into the jungle from the small path.

"All due respect sir, I don't think any of us want to rest. We want to find the guys and get the hell out of here." Said Max. Collins nodded.

"Fan out." He said. The men started to walk into the heavy foliage. Each taking out their largest knives and swinging their arms to cut down the bushes in their way. After only five minutes, one of the soldiers on the far right screamed. The others looked towards him and paused. They were frozen in fear from his blood curdling cry. Collins made his way over to the crouching soldier to see what had caused him to scream. There, under the branch of a small bush was a severed hand. It was pale, very pale, as if all the blood had been taken out. Even the cuts were bloodless. Collins used his knife to flip the hand over to see the other side. There on the wrist was a tattoo of a swallow and a date.

"Sir. Private William had that tattoo. That's the date that his son was born." The soldier said before he turned and threw up into another bush nearby. When the other soldiers heard about the tattoo they ran over to see the hand. They looked at it in horror. A soldier named James bent down.

"Sir, I studied forensics in college and there is something very wrong about this hand." James said.

"No shit James, it's a severed hand. Of course there is something wrong." Collins replied.

"No I mean, something worse." James said as he moved the hand around with his knife. These aren't cut marks. They're teeth marks. This hand was bitten off... by human teeth." The soldiers all looked to Collins. Terror spread across his face.

"Everyone back to the path." He said quietly. They stood up and ran back to the small winding path. Chris had gotten out front because he was the fastest runner they had. He was followed by Miller, Max and Collins and the rest followed them. As they ran through the silent jungle, they heard a small grunt and stopped running. Chris turned back to see that the soldier who had found the hand was gone. He blinked. His mind couldn't understand how someone could just vanish. He was about to turn back and start running again when he saw a white blur rush out from the dense jungle and tackle the second to last soldier and just like that they disappeared. Chris' eyes grew wide and he ran faster than he had ever run before. His lung burned as he finally jumped out onto the larger path.

Though he had been trained to check on his fellow soldiers, the adrenaline rush pushed him to run back to the village without turning around. He didn't stop until he got into the center of the village. Finally, he stopped running and leaned against a tree to catch his breath. He looked back toward the path and saw Miller, Max, Collins, and two others. They stopped in front of Chris and tried to catch their breath. Chris looked around.

"Where are Dave and James?" Chris asked. Collins looked up at him then looked around, still breathing hard.

"Maybe they went back to the plane already." Max coughed.

Chris didn't buy it. He looked around the grassy opening and found two pools of blood. "I don't think so." He said pointing at the blood. The others looked at each other and then flipped their heads around.

"Get back to the plane!" Collins yelled. They stood and turned to start running back to the path they had taken into the village and that is when they saw them. Blocking the path in front of them were five very pale villagers. They stood without moving or blinking. The only color on them was the red from the blood around their mouths. Their eyes were completely black and their bodies were covered in sores. Chris looked at their feet. There was dried blood on all of their feet and their fingernails were pus green.

They stood starting. The soldiers were frozen. Terrified. Slowly, the pale villagers walked towards them. Chris watched how they moved.

It was slow, clumsy movements that looked like they had lost a lot of control over their bodies.

"Well, we found the bodies..." Chris whispered. Slowly, they each pulled out their guns and rested them at their sides. "Are they...dead?" Chris asked as he quickly glanced over to Max. Max didn't respond but his jaw hung open. The look of the villagers as they walked toward the soldiers reminded them of the little girl from the ring as she crawled out of the television. It unnerved them to the very core. Miller couldn't take it. He started breathing heavy and pulled his gun up from his hip. He aimed it at the villager that was directly in front of him and pulled the trigger. He was a trained sniper and the bullet went right through the middle of the villager's forehead. It fell back ward and laid on the ground twitching for a few moments then stopped moving. The other villagers stopped walking and stood frozen once more. They all set their sights on Miller. One of the villagers finally moved. One step. It took one step forward, unhinged its jaw and let out a blood curdling hiss. In that instant, they ran towards Miller. Their speed was incredible and they ran gracefully towards their victim. It was a complete contrast to how they had walked before.

Within the blink of an eye, Miller was on the ground being torn to shreds by the villagers' teeth. Blood gushed out of everywhere and pooled below his body. The other soldiers backed away and watched the feeding frenzy. They couldn't believe what was happening. Their fellow soldier was being eaten alive in front of them. No sounds would come out of their mouths.

Collins was the first to come out of shock enough to tell them to get to the plane. Quietly, he whispered "Move out." And slowly the men backed away. When they felt they were far enough they turned and ran down the path. As they ran, they looked around them and they could see the black eyes and white faces of the undead villagers. Chris was in front. He stopped looking around and ran as fast as he could towards the plane. He heard two familiar grunts behind him and dared not look back. Finally, he saw the clearing where they had left the plane. He kicked his speed up even faster though his legs burned like acid.

He didn't stop until he had run up the cargo ramp and was inside the plane. He turned to see Max and Collins behind him. "Run!" Chris yelled. He knew that yelling wouldn't help them but he couldn't stop himself. He felt helpless and terrified. Max was running behind Collins, limping with each stride. Chris watched him and willed him to move faster but he didn't. Right on his tail was one of the undead villagers with tem more behind it. Chris watched as they gained on his best friend. He watched as they tackled him. He heard Max's cry out. He saw the red blood spread out under the pile of cannibalistic undead. Collins was still in the clear and Chris hoped that the devouring of his best friend would be enough of a distraction for Collins to make it to the plane. As Collins made his first step onto the plane ramp Chris saw a blur and Collins was gone. Chris ran to the middle of the ramp only to see a group of twenty undead villagers running towards him.

"Go! Tell them what happened. Go now!" Chris heard Collins say before the undead villagers sunk in their blood covered teeth. Chris watched as Collins was ripped apart and his flesh was ripped off his bones. He heard the sounds of teeth ripping open his throat and nails ripping open his stomach. In one moment he felt two very contradicting things. How could he leave when all of his fellow soldiers had died there? How could he leave them? But... How could he stay?

He didn't move. The internal battle waged and he was lost in the shock of the horrors he had seen. But then one of the ravenous undead looked up from Collins' mangled corpse and looked Chris dead in the eye. Chris felt his blood run cold. He turned and started to run up the ramp toward the large button that would close the belly of the plane. But the undead villager was right behind him and followed by two more. They were quick and met him when he was only three quarters of the way up the ramp. Chris whipped out his gun and shot one in the head and if tumbled back down the ramp and onto the grass by the rest of the undead. They turned to face Chris and let out hisses and moans. Chris then aimed his gun at the undead closest to him and managed to land a bullet in his chest. The white villager stopped for a moment and Chris watched to make sure he fell to the ground like the other one had.

But the undead just hissed and started towards him. Chris knew he needed to move. He needed to get closer to the button. He ran as fast as he could, hearing the heavy thumping steps behind him. He turned and pulled the trigger once more, hitting one in the head. It fell to the ground and slowly rolled down the ramp toward the other body. Chris heard more hissing but he didn't have time to look at the group of angry villagers. He bounded toward the wall that held the hatch button and turned. The third undead villager was right behind him. In less than a second, the undead villager had thrown out his arms and shoved Chris against the metal wall. Chris felt the sting of pain flow through his back. He saw the white villager up close. He could smell the blood on his breath and it mixed with the rotting scent that came from the undead villager's skin.

The undead was waxy looking. Like it was sweating. Its eyes never blinked as it threw its hands out to scrape Chris. Chris' adrenaline went into over drive. He moved quicker than he ever had before in his life. He jumped out just out of reach then sent a front kick into the chest of the undead with the greatest force he could muster. The villager stumbled back then hissed. It jumped back with its teeth gnawing at the air and landed right in front of Chris, sinking its teeth into his forearm. The pain was excruciating but Chris' mind was clear and in survival mode. As the Zombie bit into his arm, he used his other to pull up his gun and shoot the undead in the head. Instantly, it fell to the ground. It twitched for a moment then became still. Using what was left of his adrenaline, Chris quickly hit the button to close the ramp and then threw the body out to a group of hissing villagers.

He saw them try to climb onto the closing ramp. He saw white arms and legs through the cracks. Once he heard the familiar thud of the ramp closing, he ran to the cockpit. He silently thanked Collins for forcing him to take flying lessons for the past two years even though he had hated flying. He hit all the switches and heard the plane hum to life. As he checked all of his levels and metrics he heard loud thuds against the sides of the plane. He knew the undead were hitting it, still trying to get in. He buckled his seatbelt, as he had a thousand times and started to turn the plane so he could take off over the nearby cliff. He knew that was his fastest way of getting in the air. As he turned, he looked out the large windows in front of him. He listened as the thudding sounds moved along the side of the plane. Then he saw the white limbs of the undead. They were climbing on top of the plane. If they got to the windows, they could break them and Chris would be stuck there. He tried to swing the plane around to shake them off but they held on tight. His best bet would be to take off and have them fall off from the immense speed.

He looked ahead. He had just enough land before the cliff to get enough momentum but only if he floored it. He said a silent prayer. The first prayer he had said in many years. Then he put on his head set and pushed the wheel forward. The engine roared, drowning out the sounds of the thudding. And then he was going. He was bumbling across the uneven grassy plain towards the cliff. He pushed forward as hard as he could. To his horror, the undead had made it onto the nose of the plane and were making their way to the glass. Just as he reached the cliff, one of the undead had his fist pulled back ready to strike the glass. The plane rolled off and dove towards the sea below. Chris pulled up as hard as he could watching all the undead villagers fall off the front of the plane.

Sirens were buzzing and beeping as he plummeted towards the sea. He pulled up with all his might, ignoring the pain of the bite in his forearm. Just before he hit the water, the plane leveled out and he pulled up. With a sigh of relief he climbed in altitude and set his trajectory to Okinawa. Once he was at his cruising altitude he left the cockpit to find a bandage for his arm. In the first aid kit he found bandages and rubbing alcohol. He brought them back to the cock pit and sat down in one of the chairs. He took off his army jacket and saw his would for the first time. It was a deep bite but the weird part was that it wasn't swollen or red. It just looked like someone had bitten him and his body hadn't reacted. He bit down on the sleeve of his thick jacket and pour the rubbing alcohol over his arm. To his surprise there was little pain. He bandaged his arm and returned to the pilot's seat. For the duration of his flight, he did everything he could to not think of what he had just seen. The memories flashed through his brain despite his best efforts and he went through waves of crying, screaming in horror and feeling numb.

Finally, he saw the little island he called home. He had hoped that it would bring him relief but he felt only small reassurance. As he neared their airspace he was greeted by the air traffic control tower.

"Hey boys welcome back." Said a cheery unknowing voice over the headset.

"This is Chris Muscovy from Unit 311 requesting emergency landing." Chris said as clearly as he could.

"Oh..." The voice responded, surprised by his request. "Landing strip two is cleared for you. You are a go for emergency landing."

Chris always hated this part. Landing had always given him a nervous feeling but now, he felt nothing. He landed the plane as he had a hundred times but this time with no fear. When he pulled the plane to a stop, he just sat there. He didn't move, he didn't rush to get off the plane. What was he going to say? What would he tell them about the other men?

Finally the ramp opened and four soldiers came in. They looked around for other passengers before approaching him.

"Where are the others?" They asked. Chris just sat there. The soldiers noticed his bandaged arm and decided to leave him there. They went back to base camp to get one of the sergeants. The man that Collins had been in contact with came back out with two medics. They approached Chris slowly.

"Chris... We are going to take you to the infirmary and while the medics look you over, you can tell me what happened ok?" The Sergeant said soothingly. When Chris didn't move, the medics looked at each other then they looked at the sergeant. He nodded and they stepped forward to each side of Chris to help him up. As soon as they touched him he screamed and jumped up. The medics were startled and jumped back. Chris turned to face the Sergeant.

"It's ok now, Chris, you're safe." He said. Chris was breathing heavy and there was panic in his eyes. One of the medics stepped up behind him and stuck a needle in his back. It was a sedative. Within seconds, Chris slunk back in the chair and the medics were able to carry him to a wheel chair that sat at the bottom of the ramp. As they wheeled him away, the sergeant noticed the dents in the side of the plane that had been made by the villagers.

When Chris came to, he was in his own room in the infirmary. He blinked and looked around at the pale green walls and the two way mirror that were directly in front of him. He felt exhausted. The adrenaline had left his body raw and every muscle felt heavy. Every muscle except for those near the bite in his arm. His arm had a new bandage on it and he traced it with his other hand. Then, he adjusted his bed so he was in more of a seated position. Just then, the door opened and the same sergeant walked in.

"Chris. I know you are very tired but I need to know what happened. Where are the others?" The sergeant asked. Chris looked down. He didn't want to talk about what he had seen but he knew they needed to know so that they could do something to get rid of those haunting creatures.

"At first, we just saw blood. Large pools of it. Then we saw human foot prints. We looked for the bodies but we couldn't find any. We went into the jungle and that's when... that's when they started disappearing." He said as he started to shake.

"Who disappeared?" The sergeant asked.

"The other soldiers. We split into groups of four. One never came back. We sent in another group to get them. Only one came back, he was out of his mind. Then we all went in. We found the pools of blood and the foot prints and then... a hand." He stopped. He could see it so clearly. Clear as if he was still back in that jungle. "It was completely white and there was no blood in it. But it had a tattoo on it and we knew it was one of the missing soldiers... the worst part..." He paused, feeling very sick. "There were human bite marks on it. We ran as fast as we could but by time we got back to the village there were only a few of us left. That's when we saw them."

"Saw who? The bodies?" The sergeant asked. Chris shook his head.

"They were the villagers but they weren't... they were pale and their eyes were black. They we slow, then they were fast. They ate them! All of them!" Chris screamed and wailed.

The sergeant looked at him in surprise. This was not what he was expecting and he wasn't sure if he should believe Chris or if Chris had some sort of mental break. The sergeant watch Chris as he brought his hands up to his head and tried to shake the horrors out. That's when he noticed something that convinced him. Chris' hand, the one attached to the bandaged forearm, was completely white. He backed away and Chris looked up at him as he moved. His eyes, the irises, were black and the whites of his eyes were yellow.

"Chris... how are you feeling?" The sergeant asked slowly. Chris looked down at his hand to see its paleness.

"No. no. no. no!" He screamed. Chris clawed at his hand and realized he had no sensation in it though he had complete control over its movements. "Cut it off!" He screamed and thrashed around on his bed. The sergeant ran out of the room and locked the door. He walked into the room to look at Chris through the two way mirror. Chris flailed around and thrashed on his bed screaming for ten minutes. Finally, the Sergeant ordered for a medic to give him another sedative. Four medics went in to hold him down and one gave him another shot. As his body relaxed they left him and relocked the door.

"Shut off the lights, let him sleep. Let's see if the CDC has any idea what this could be. We will keep him sedated until we have a cure." The sergeant said.

"Yes sir." One of the soldiers in the room replied as he turned off the lights. Another soldier called the CDC to start the process of air mailing a vaccination and the Sergeant began making calls to the Vietnamese military to explain the real effects of the chemical weapon. He instructed them to evacuate the nearby villages immediately but they were giving him a lot of excuses.

"I understand that..." The sergeant said into the phone. "But they are in real danger and this could turn into an epidemic.... I know that it costs money to relocate people but if you leave them there you are basically sentencing them to death... I don't know if there is a cure... I see. Fine." He hung up. He picked up the phone to call Washington DC.

"Yes we have a potential hazard in Vietnam. My boys went out to check this morning. Only one came back... President Quan is unresponsive to my suggestions... Yes sir... we have the boy in the infirmary now. In a locked room.... We are working with the CDC... Yes sir." And he hung up. The sergeant leaned over to check something on the monitor in front of him. Then a noise came from the dark room in front of them. The sergeant stood up from his chair and walked to the mirror. He couldn't see much because the room was so dark. But then they heard another noise. The other soldiers stood and walked over to the mirrored window too.

"Turn on the lights Ed." He said.

"Yes sir." Said the soldier closest to the switch. He flipped it and the soldiers jumped back in horror. There standing directly in front of the sergeant, staring through the two way mirror, was Chris. A very pale, black eyed, drooling version of Chris. His IV had been ripped out and his bed was upside down and shoved against one of the walls. He was so close to the glass that the sergeant could see his hot rotting breath fog the glass.

"Dear God." The sergeant exclaimed quietly as he stared back at the undead soldier. He wanted to know if Chris could see through the mirror. He waved his hand close to the glass and Chris' black eyes shifted to the movement. The sergeant stopped and turned pale in fear.

"We need to shoot him!" One of the soldiers yelled, but the sergeant was frozen. Just then, in one swift motion, the undead soldier drew back his fist and landed it on the glass, shattering it as if it was a thin vase.

"Shoot him! Shoot him! Shoot him!"

Those were the last words the Sergeant heard before he died.

THE SOUND OF ZOMBIES by George De La Torre

The radio static faded in and out mixing with the sounds of the stations as Todd turned the dial to the right frequency. Sue Ann listened intently, trying to hear the familiar voice who broadcast the afternoon news. Finally Todd stopped moving the dial and the group of friends pulled up their lawn chairs close enough to listen to the half hour broadcast. Bobby had just walked up with five glasses of his moonshine when the program began.

"Hello listeners, welcome to today's program. I am Monica Robbins, the host of 'Today, Right Now'. For those of you who are new to the program, we want to welcome you to a broadcast that is devoted to keeping you informed on the news from our fallen country and from the rest of the world. Now we bring you 'Today, Right Now'. September 15th, 2058. With the help of the Mexican government at our southern border, the Infected Human problem has been completely wiped out of the Western half of the country. In a new treaty with Mexico, we have given back land from Texas to California that will drastically change the landscape of this country. More British and French forces have arrived in New York and Florida to help stabilize the regions before moving further into the Midwest. They have brought supplies and machinery to help rebuilt the Unites States' factories and farms. The drought in California has yet to see relief and our nation's current state is not equip to assist the Californian farms. The president released news today of a task force made up of the remaining CIA and FBI agents who will begin checking state by state for any Infected Human populations. The task force did a test run of their mission and cleared Massachusetts of any Infected Human Corpses. The task force then set up a new police team and trained them to continue to search. Their goal is to have New England cleared within three weeks. Residents seem hopeful and most haven't had contact with an Infected Human corpse in months. The last sighting nationwide is believed to be in Northern Kentucky. In other news, China has invaded the Eastern province of Russia and seem to have very little opposition. The Russian Govern..."

Todd flicked off the radio and leaned back against his chair. Mary Beth shot up from her chair, "Hey! I wanted to hear that Todd." She whined.

"Why do you care about Russia? It ain't got nothing to do with us. Besides didn't you hear what she said? The last Zombie sighting was here in Kentucky. Don't cha think maybe we ought to figure out what to do about it? It might be the last one. If we kill it, then we can start rebuildin' our lives." He said in an annoyed voice. Mary Beth slumped back in her chair and pouted.

"So what should we do?" Sue Ann asked. Bobby smiled and leaned toward her.

"We gotta hunt it down an' kill it." He said with a laugh. Sue Ann rolled her eyes.

"Yea? And how we gonna do that when we don't know where in Kentucky it is or if it's even still here?" She asked poking him in the ribs.

"They said Northern Kentucky. We know that the Zombies tend to stay in the forests until they are hungry enough to hunt." Todd said.

"Oh. Why didn't you say so? And since there is only one forest in Northern Kentucky we can find him no problem." Sue Ann said sarcastically. Todd glared at her but knew that she was right.

"Why don't we set it a trap?" Joe said quietly. The other four looked at him in surprise. Joe didn't talk much. He had seen too many horrible things since the outbreak and silence was his way of dealing with it. The others had changed too. Each had their own way of making sense of it. Bobby made it into a hunting game. Todd had out bursts of rage mixed with general unpleasantness, Sue Ann had long since blocked off any emotions and Mary Beth pretended that her world hadn't changed. The five of them never talked about the past. They avoided discussing any dead relatives or friends and they never talked about the future. For so long it had been too uncertain. Now there was hope. Though each of his friends were acting like everything was going to be normal, he could see desperation on their faces.

"What kind of trap?" Bobby said with a coy smile.

"Well, it will come out when it's hungry and will attack the first human it sees. We can track it enough by looking for its left over meals and then trick it by parading a buffet of human flesh in front of it." Joe explained. Bobby smiled.

"Why do we have to kill it? Why don't we just let someone else do it? It's too risky." Said Mary Beth. She was scared and had the right to be. She had watched her little sister get eaten in front of her by the zombies. She wanted to stay as far away from them as she could.

Bobby turned to her. "Are you kidding? And let someone else be the hero who rid the world of Zombies for good? I don't think so. I want to kill the last one myself."

Joe nodded. "I agree with Bobby. I want to know that it's over first hand. The sooner we kill it, the sooner this is all a distant memory."

Todd slammed his glass down on the arm of his chair. His friends were so used to it that they didn't even flinch. "Let's get the son of a bitch." Then they all looked at Sue Ann. Sue Ann looked at Mary Beth and saw the fear in her eyes. But she had lost her ability to empathize. She knew that Mary Beth had a point. If it wasn't them, it would be someone else. It was only a matter of time. But really what was there to be afraid of. Their lives had been over for years. Sue Ann wasn't suicidal but she also looked at her life objectively. There was no pleasure left in it. There was nothing real to hold on to. She shrugged.

"Whatever." She said plainly. The three boys cheered and Mary Beth hung her head in her hands. The guys planned the trap and discussed the supplies they would need and how to get them. Mary Beth let tears roll down her cheek for a moment then turned the radio pack on to catch the rest of the program. Sue Ann just looked out over the rolling hills of long green grass. They had been living out of an abandoned farm house out in the countryside. She remembered the first day they got there. She was shaking but felt nothing. Todd and Bobby had helped her into what was now her bedroom and kept asking the same thing. "Are you ok?"

She heard them ask her at least ten times but their voices had been fuzzy. What did Ok mean? Did she know what it meant that morning? Before it happened. She and her boyfriend, Rick, were getting supplies from a looted store when the attack happened. Out of nowhere four Zombies were walking towards them. Sue Ann's boyfriend fought them off while she escaped and ran for the car. Rick jumped in the driver's seat and slammed the door, not moments after Sue Ann had buckled her seatbelt. He sped off down the road and lost the zombies easily. Though they could run surprisingly fast, they weren't as fast as a car.

But that's when it started. He coughed a few times. Then he threw up blood on the steering wheel. Sue Ann knew in that moment what was happening. She saw a small bite on his arm. He pulled over and looked at her with terror and fear in his eyes. Through the blood oozing from his mouth he managed to say, "Shoot me in the head." She hesitated and he slammed his hand on the dash. "Do it!" He choked. She pulled out the gun and ammo that they had just stolen from the store and put it on her lap. She didn't know if she could make herself shoot him. The gun was loaded and heavy in her hands. She looked him in the eyes and remembered all the good times they had had together and how much she loved him. She started to put the gun away when Rick let out an unearthly growl and gnashed his teeth at her. Without thinking, she raised the gun and shot him squarely in the forehead. Survival mode had kicked in. She opened his door and pushed his limp body out onto the road and took his place in the driver's seat. She managed to drive to the meet up place before going into shock. She recovered her faculties but remained numb to any feelings.

Sue Ann looked out across the farm land and wondered what would happen to her once they killed the last Zombie. Would she feel again or would she be like this forever? The sunset and Bobby grilled up some deer meat from his last hunting excursion. One thing he appreciated about the zombie epidemic was that hunting laws were null and void. That night, each of the five friends laid awake wondering what this hunt would mean and what they would do when this was over. It was the first time since the beginning of the epidemic that they had even considered life after this.

The next morning, they loaded up the Ford truck with supplies and headed out. Joe drove and the girls sat in the cab with him. Bobby and Todd sat in the bed of the truck and watched for large animals they could shoot. They had decided to start in the part of the forest that was closest to a small town. The reported sighting had come from one of the locals and the friends figured that the zombie wouldn't stray too far from the easy hunting ground. When they arrived in the small town they stopped at the store. Many small stores had reopened selling what it could manage to get. Every single store they went to, Todd would check for potato chips.

"Finally! See this trip is a great idea already." Todd sang as he ripped open his chips. Sue Ann and Mary Beth both rolled their eyes but little smiles spread across their face. They knew that Todd was much easier to be around when he was in a good mood. They didn't care if it was chips or shooting at trees. They indulged him when they could. "Alright, let's do this!" He yelled and Joe took the dirt road to the entrance to the state park and forest. They pulled in and immediately saw rows of abandoned cars. Most of the cars had plants growing around them and looked like they had been there for a while.

Some of the car doors were open and picnic baskets were haphazardly strewn on the ground. It looked like a time capsule. From the way the cars were parked and which doors were open, it looked like there was a massive attack and the zombies killed all of the park goers at once. But there were no bodies. Somehow, Mary Beth felt like it was much creepier without bodies. They all walked slowly through the parking lot. They checked each car to make sure nothing was hiding.

Wind blew through the trees above making the branches dance a melancholy dance over the car graveyard. *Slam!* The car door from the chevy behind them slammed shut making Mary Beth and Todd jump out of fear.

"It's just the wind." Sue Ann said flatly. Mary Beth stared at the car door. Something didn't feel right and the hair began to stand up of the back of her neck. She felt something watching her. She looked around but couldn't see anything. Bobby, who had been talking loudly quieted down too. Each of the five felt the same eerie presence. They looked around in every direction and behind every car but they couldn't find anything or anyone. They tried to shake the feeling but they couldn't. Bobby looked at Todd and said, "Maybe it's time we got our guns?"

Todd's mood had changed dramatically from his euphoric experience with the chips. "Yea, let's just find the damn thing and shoot it." All five of them headed to the car. Each chose a different kind of gun and took the matching ammo.

"Alright, I say we search the perimeter of the parking lot. That way we will find any trails they may have created." Said Bobby and the rest nodded. They split up in two groups. They walked slowly around each side until they met at the far end of the parking lot.

"We didn't see anything..." Said Todd. Sue Ann looked around them and noticed something. There was a swarm of flies coming from a tall patch of grass at the bottom of a nearby tree. She grabbed Todd's arm. "What's that?" She said pointing. She and Todd walked over and found a bloody human leg. It had been gnawed off at the knee and was still wearing a tennis shoe. The blood looked pretty fresh. Fear washed over the group as the reality of their hunt sunk in.

"It looks like it's already eating." Said Joe. Bobby looked at the leg then noticed a trail of blood leading away from it and farther into the forest.

"Yea and we have a trail." He said pointing at the blood. He took a step forward to follow the blood trail when Mary Beth grabbed his arm.

"You said we were setting a trap, not wandering through the forest hoping he doesn't find us first. I say we make the trap here. It's obvious that he will hunt here." She said with overwhelming fear in her voice.

"Yeah but look at the leg. It's fresh which means the zombie just ate. They can go a week without eating again. I ain't waiting that long." He said as he started off into the forest. Mary Beth looked at Todd and Joe. They both shrugged.

"We have a better chance of killing this thing and staying safe if we stay together. Just think of how you will feel tonight knowing that there are no more zombies." Joe reasoned. Then he started to follow Bobby. Sue Ann followed Joe and Todd walked behind her taking Mary Beth's arm in his.

"Come on. It will be over soon." He said in an uncharacteristically kind voice.

As they walked the trees became denser which blocked out a lot of the sunlight. It was darker and felt cooler. Mary Beth seemed to be more effected by the changes than the others and began shivering. After about ten minutes Bobby stopped suddenly. He found the lower part of an arm. It seemed to match the skin tone of the leg they had found and the trail of blood continued. The smell of the rotting flesh wafted up to their noses and they coughed and quickly covered their noses. They stared at it. They wondered why the zombie hadn't eaten the flesh from the arm or the leg.

"Why do you think the zombie left pieces behind?" Todd asked. He was obviously freaked out by the trail of limps. Usually the Infected Human Corpses ate everything. They had never seen a zombie leave behind things they could eat.

"Maybe this person didn't taste good." Bobby joked. No one laughed. Mary Beth just glared at him and the smile disappeared from his face. Sue Ann crouched down to look at the arm. There was a tattoo on the wrist and its nails were yellow and chipping.

"I think this person was sick. Maybe Infected Human Corpses can't eat people with a specific illness. I wonder what they had..." She said leaning over the arm to get a closer look. Suddenly, the arm jerked and wiggled on the ground. In a snake like motion it squirmed over to Sue Ann's leg. They all screamed and ran back towards the parking lot. When they ran past the place where they had found the leg, they noticed that it was gone.

When they reached the parking lot the stood in a circle in an open area. After they huffed and puffed from the running, Sue Ann stood upright. "I think the person who was eaten was already infected with the IHC virus. Maybe, they were somehow immune to it turning them into a zombie but when the zombie tried to eat them, their limbs reacted to the virus."

"And this matters how?" Todd said through his gasps. "Knowing what it is eating doesn't help us. We just need to find it and kill it."

"Well I know one thing for sure. I am not going back in that way." Said Joe. Bobby turned back to look at the forest.

"Fine we can go around from the road. But we gotta go now. It looks like a storm is rolling in." He said pointing to the dark sky. The group of friends walked down the dirt road they had driven in on and turned right at the fork in the road. After a half an hour walk, they found a walking path that jutted into the forest. Bobby headed in first again and the others followed keeping an eye out for body parts. They didn't find any but they did see bloody handprints on the trees that lined the path. They pressed on. After seeing an increasing number of bloody hand prints and trails of blood droplets in the dirt, Mary Beth was thoroughly creeped out. That is when she noticed that the wind had stopped. The trees were perfectly still and the air grew stale.

"Guys..." She said quietly. But before she could point out the change in weather she saw a dark blurry figure tackle Bobby and drag him into the trees. He screamed for only a matter of seconds as his friends listened in horror. The screams turned to the sound of him choking on blood. Todd screamed and ran back the other direction and the same blur grabbed him and dragged him off into the dense greenery. The remaining three friends ran deeper into the woods as fast as they could. Joe was in the lead and ran faster than he ever had in his life. Soon he happened upon a small cottage that was used to store the park equipment. Luckily, he found that the door was unlocked and he jumped inside. He watched through a crack in the door until he say Mary Beth and Sue Ann run by. Quickly he grabbed them and pulled them into the cottage.

They stood in the dark room breathing hard. Joe locked the door from the inside and made sure that they were away from the windows. No one knew what to say. Mary Beth was crying and Sue Ann just stared at the floor. Mary Beth's sobs grew louder and louder. Joe stepped forward and put his hand over her mouth. "Shshhhhhhh" he said quietly.

She blinked hard then looked at him and nodded. She tried to calm herself as best she could. The horror of the rapid attack replayed in her mind over and over. "They were just gone. They were just gone." She repeated quietly over and over.

Joe looked at her then at Sue Ann. "I guess he was still hungry." He said. Mary Beth looked at him in shock.

"Do you think this is funny?" She hissed.

He shook his head. "No, not at all. I only said that because it doesn't make sense. Every single zombie attack we know about, the Zombies attack enough to kill one person. Feeding off one person usually lasts them for a few days. They only attack out of hunger. But this one is attacking for another reason." He trailed off.

Sue Ann turned toward him. "They don't have reasons. It's their base instinct to attack for food. They don't think about it or anything." She spat.

"This one might." He said. Mary Beth's eyes grew wide. Sue Ann shook her head refusing to believe him.

"No, no. Maybe they are more like animals than we thought. Animals kill for two reasons, they are hungry or they feel threatened." She hypothesized. Before Joe could make another argument he saw something out of the corner of his eye. He turned toward the window to see a bloody corpse staring at him. He stopped cold. The girls turned to the window and froze in fear. Slowly the Zombie backed away from the window and walked around the cottage toward the door. Joe immediately turned his eyes to the door knob. The girls gasped as they watch the knob twist. Zombies didn't have reasoning skills. They shouldn't know how to open a door. Joe was glad he had been extra cautious in locking it behind him.

When the door didn't budge the zombie pushed harder. Soon, the cottage was filled with the sounds of the zombie screaming and wailing in frustration. Then the wailing stopped and it got quiet. The three friends could hear each other breathing. They looked at each other and then looked toward the window. Joe slowly made his way over to look out. When he got close enough, he peered out through the glass window to see the zombie standing 4 feet from the door staring at it. Then, with one quick step, the zombie threw itself at the locked door creating a crack in the wood.

"Quickly!" Sue Ann screamed as she began piling the park equipment in front of the door. They put shelves, tables and large metal tools at the base of the door. The pile rattled each time the zombie threw itself at the other side of the door. The three friends sat with their backs to the pile in order to add extra support to their barricade. The screeching sounds coming from the hysterical zombie flooded the cottage and the three covered their ears.

After what seemed to be an hour, the screeching stopped and so did the banging.

"Is it gone?" Mary Beth asked as she shook in fear. Sue Ann just looked at her. The blood had drained from her face and she looked paler than the moon.

"I don't know. But something is different. He tried to open the door with the handle. They shouldn't be able to do that." Joe said.

"If there is something different with this one... if he is able to use reasoning then what happens next?" Sue Ann asked. She looked at Mary Beth and Joe. They seemed equally lost. "What if it didn't kill Todd and Bobby for food or out of fear?" Sue said after a while. Joe and Mary Beth looked up at her not knowing where she was going with this.

"What other reasons could it have?" Joe asked. Sue Ann shrugged. Just then a rustling noise came from outside the front of the cabin. All three immediately turned toward the noise. Then another sound came from behind the back of the cabin and they flipped their heads around. *Thump!* A sound came from the roof. They all looked up. Then Sue Ann grabbed Joe's arm.

"What if it knew that it was the last one... and it's... recruiting..." She said slowly. The other two looked at her with new terror in their eyes. Just then they saw Todd in the window with blood dripping from his mouth and a dead look in his eyes. At the other window they saw a flash of movement and then saw Bobby's eyes piercing through the glass as he gnashed his teeth. *Crack!* The roof gave in and the zombie was standing in front of them. Slowly, he walked over to the pile of stuff in front of the door. With incredible strength, he pushed it aside and opened the door for the other two fresh zombies. They slowly entered the cottage and cornered Joe, Sue Ann and Mary Beth.

Before he felt the sting of the bite, Joe whispered, "but it was almost over." The three died to the sound of teeth on their bones. They were spotted in town three weeks later.

They were the start of the second epidemic.

ZOMBIES DON'T CRY by Matthew Pierce

CHAPTER ONE

"Do it, Ray," she said with a dark look in her eyes, "just do it!"

With hypnotized eyes, he stared at the long knife in his hand. The silver length of the cold blade felt strange and deadly as he ran his fingers over it...the whole thing seemed almost unreal and he looked down again at Cindy Stone. She lay there in the middle of the pentagram; a red hood drawn over her pretty face and her long black hair totally obscured from sight.

"Chiagon chiagon ros soth-oth!" she shouted and something took complete hold of his mind when he heard those words. He suddenly found himself in a strange twilight between life and death where he could still recall some of the events that had lead up to that point, yet he was totally unable to call upon his reason to control his actions any longer.

It was supposed to be just another weekend away with the rest of his biker gang "The Zombies" and he'd been looking forward to three days of unadulterated sex and orgies in the woods. All of the members of The Zombies motorcycle club had arrived at Thompson Creek Woods the previous evening. It had been a Friday night, with a full moon, and the activities of the first evening did not disappoint. Ray could still vividly recall the drunken sexual pleasures he'd shared with Cindy and the other biker members of the club the previous evening. All of the bikers in his gang had dabbled in the occult and they all had an interest in dark rituals, but most of them, including Ray Mason, only really used these occult practices as a means of enslaving young girls to the group and having sex orgies with them.

Ray had slept well and started drinking early that morning, even though the sun had scarcely reached a decent spot in the sky before he reached for the whiskey bottle. When Cindy insisted on taking him for a walk through the woods so early in the day he didn't make much of it and thought, "What the fuck, let's take a walk and see what this gorgeous biker chick has in mind. Probably just some new twisted sexual way of getting off, he'd thought as they winded their way down the barely visible path through the dense trees.

They eventually got to a clearing and Ray immediately noticed the pentagram that was carved out on the large rock which protruded from the moist ground, right in the middle of the open space.

"Nice spot for some private sexual ritual," he'd joked when they came to a halt in the middle of the clearing.

Cindy looked at him with her dark seductive eyes. She had the facial features of an ancient warrior princess and her body was both muscular and incredibly feminine. That much Ray Mason could personally vouch for, having spent some very intimate and naked moments with her the previous night. Cindy didn't say a word and produced a small radio from her backpack. He'd expected some heavy metal rock music to blare through the early morning skies as she switched on the power, but instead, the most hauntingly beautiful violin music filled the silence. Cindy slowly undressed herself to the sound and rhythm of the enchanting music and soon she was swaying to and fro, completely naked in front of his mesmerized eyes.

"Come dance with me, Ray," she invited with a sweetness in her voice that was way too innocent to be true.

"I'm glad you brought me out here for this private little ritual," he'd whispered in her ear as they ran their hands over each other's naked bodies and danced to the slow violin music. The first sign that this was not just some overly romantic manifestation of an enamored female mind was when Cindy reached for her backpack and produced a bright red robe, which she stepped into with losing her rhythm. Ray had seen one of these satanic robes before in a movie, but the level of his interest in the occult had simply not been high enough for him to go to the trouble of getting one for himself.

"Nice, I like," he whispered and swayed with her to the beat of the music. There was something absolutely mesmerizing about the whole thing and Ray could feel his heart beating like a drum inside his chest.

"Do you want me, Ray?" Cindy asked and in that moment he knew that he wanted her more than he'd ever wanted anything in is life. Never mind the fact that he'd already fucked her a hundred times on these biker outings; this whole set up was so different and so sensually irresistible that he couldn't bear the thought of not having her all to himself right there and then.

"Yes I do and I'm gonna take you right now," he'd whispered with the cocky self-assurance that only the leader of a vicious biker gang could possibly muster.

"But that means nothing Ray...after all I've had sex with many of the other bikers in this motorcycle club...I mean, do you want all of me forever and ever...all to yourself?"

"Yes I do," he'd answered without thinking.

"Would you give your life to be with me forever?"

"Yes I would," he said and from that moment on every move they made had taken on a different, ancient meaning. He was no longer the master of his senses. Cindy reached into her backpack and produced a large marijuana joint. She lit it and they both inhaled deeply as they took turns smoking it. When Cindy produced another bright red hood and insisted that he put it on, he hadn't so much as blinked. Ray Mason wasn't in control anymore and he'd been reduced, for the moment, to being Cindy's obedient slave. The vicious leader of The Zombies biker club leaned back against the large rock and watched in morbid fascination as Cindy produced a black book from her backpack and started reading from its contents. He couldn't understand any of the words she read, but each sentence had sent a cold chill down his spine.

"Geagin rabando sexterenas...contraribus retendo sachendos!"

"What the fuck are you reading?" he'd asked after one particularly ominous sounding sentence.

"Just some beautiful words to prepare us for the crossing," Cindy smiled and kept reading from the strange book.

"Here, now you read us some of the poetry," Cindy said and handed him the book. "The Satanic Bible in Ancient Latin by Anton LaVey," it said on the cover and Ray could still remember that he, for a fleeting moment, felt like throwing the book as far as he could and running for his life.

"It's just some poetry...come on read to me Ray," Cindy said and when he looked into her sweet dark eyes all thoughts of resistance melted away.

"Machissimo omnes credentialis" he read and the words rolled off his tongue and cut through his mind like some long forgotten voices from the past.

"That was beautiful...now let me read you some more while you hold this for me," Cindy said and handed him an ancient sacrificial knife. She took the book and read some more of its enchanting contents while he looked at the knife from all angles.

"If you really want me forever you will have to sacrifice both of us on this rock," Cindy announced and for some reason, her words made absolute and perfect sense to him. "But before we proceed there is something we have to put on," she said and took two necklaces with ornamental crosses from her backpack. She put one of the necklaces around his neck and slipped the other one over her own neck.

"I thought that was only for vampires," Ray said, but Cindy didn't even blink an eyelid at his attempted joke.

"Do this and we will be together forever...I promise you we will never ever die as long as we wear these crosses," she whispered and Ray nodded his head. He stared at her the way a deer stares at the oncoming lights of a truck in the night.

I'm gonna lie down now...I want you to take me over the crossing first...do you know what to do?" Cindy asked and looked at him from the dangerous depths of her dark eyes.

"Yes. I take you first and then I follow you to the other side where we will be together forever," he answered and Cindy nodded her head.

"Put it through my heart and then fall into it yourself," she said and Ray looked up at the clear blue sky one last time. Then he lifted the blade high above his head with both hands. He hesitated for a moment before he brought down the knife with deadly force.

The blade penetrated Cindy's heart and she let out a blood-curdling scream before looking into his eyes one last time.

"I'll be waiting for you," she said and then blew out her final breath.

"I will be with you just now," Ray Mason whispered and fell into the sharp steel of the sacrificial blade. The handle of the blade stopped dead against the rock surface and the other end cut through Ray's heart in an instant. The pain was incredible and shot through his body like a lightning bolt. He rolled over on his back and watched as the blue skies above his head slowly turned black.

Then it all faded away and Ray fell next to Cindy's inanimate body in the middle of the clearing.

CHAPTER TWO

They looked at one another with slight surprise and for a second the whole thing seemed like it had only been a bad dream. It was getting dark already and Ray realized that they must have been lying in the clearing for a couple of hours.

"We made it...how do you feel?" Cindy asked and Ray's mind took a moment longer than usual to interpret the words. He ran his fingers across his face and his flesh felt cold to his touch.

"I can't feel anything," he answered and looked at Cindy's empty eyes. She was still beautiful and her body still looked inviting, yet Ray felt absolutely no sexual desire for her anymore. Instead, he felt that a bite of her flesh would be delicious. The only thing that stopped him, for some reason which his mind couldn't quite fathom, from taking a hold of her and feasting on her body was the cross she had around her neck.

"Whatever you do don't take off your cross," Cindy said and he nodded his head.

"I have enough crosses in my bag for all the other bikers of our club," she added and looked at Ray to see if he'd understood her meaning. Ray nodded his head again and looked at the knife where it had fallen to the ground after their ritual.

"You and me baby, we will start a brand new biker's club," he said in a cold, deadly voice.

They walked back to the place where the rest of the bikers had been camped out and stopped far enough away from the camp to make sure that their presence remained a secret to the other bikers. A couple of the rough looking bikers were sitting around a fire and it was clear from their slurred speech that they were already drunk.

"Where the fuck is Ray and Cindy?" one of the bikers asked and handed the bottle of Tequila in his hand to the topless girl next to him.

"Forget about those two and come take care of these two," the girl said and shook her tits to make her point.

Soon the two of them were both naked and Ray watched dispassionately as they kissed and started another biker orgy. Two other girls joined in the fun and some heavily tattooed male bikers also got rid of their clothes.

Cindy looked at Ray. "Only take one bite or they will not cross over," she said and Ray, even though his mind was working slower than before, understood her instruction.

"We will eat well when everyone has made the crossing," Cindy whispered and the two of them lay there watching the strange spectacle of drunken bikers having sex.

Jenny Fuller, a pretty young student, had been riding hard on top of Jerry Fallon, an ex-convict and gangster from downtown Los Angeles for about twenty minutes and finally got off him to announce that she needed to take a leak in the bushes.

"Don't worry, I will keep your spot for you," Angela Brown said with a naughty grin and climbed on top of Jerry as soon as Jenny started walking to the dark bushes surrounding the clearing.

"You take her, I want to have me some man meat," Cindy whispered and Ray started crawling slowly to the place where he'd seen Jenny enter the bushes. He crawled through some thorny patches and even when a sharp stone cut through the skin on his right knee Ray felt no pain. His vision was clear and his mind was sending a determined message to his body. He was determined to take Jenny and nothing was going to stop him.

Ray saw Jenny sitting behind a green shrub with her back towards him. Her bare back was white in the light of the moon and she was totally unaware of his presence. The strange words which Cindy had been reading to Ray earlier, before their crossing, were now thundering through his mind and he somehow fully understood their secret meaning.

With one final stretch, Ray crawled to within five feet of Jenny. His hands made a scraping noise as he got to his feet and Jenny jumped to her feet in shocked surprise.

"What the fuck...oh, it's only you Ray," she said when she saw Ray standing in front of her, "why are your eyes so red, have you been mainlining heroin again?"

"Crossed over, taking you with me too," Ray said and Jenny laughed out loud.

"Yip, you've definitely been shooting some strong shit up your veins," she said and then Ray grabbed her with cold, deadly hands around her throat. She tried to scream but his grip was like steel and the last things she saw was his open mouth before he sank his teeth into her face and tore out a large chunk of flesh out of it. A strange sensation rushed through her body as she died and regained consciousness again, almost immediately. It felt as if some strange poison had been administered to her system and she felt alive and dead all at once. Ray let her go and stood back to look at her maimed face. There was a large hole in her left cheek and it should have hurt, but for some reason she felt almost grateful to Ray for what he'd done. She couldn't feel anything and her mind was devoid of the troubling emotions that seemed to haunt her when she was still human. All she felt now was a desire to eat some human flesh and she would have jumped right on top of the leader of The Zombies to take a bite out of him, were it not for the foreboding cross that she saw around his neck.

"Here, you will need this," Ray said and took a necklace with a cross from the pocket of the strange red robe he was wearing. It took all of Ray's efforts not to simply rip the rest of Jenny's flesh right off her bones. He hung the cross around her neck and repeated the instructions that Cindy had given to him.

"We first get all the other members and then we eat well. For now only take one bite," he ordered and Jenny nodded her head. Her thoughts were focused, even though the rate at which they traveled through her mind had slowed down considerably. When Cindy saw Ray and Jenny approaching she looked pleased. She ran her cold eyes over Jenny's face and noticed the bloody wound where Ray had taken his deadly bite.

"We'll get your clothes when all the others have crossed over," she said to Jenny and Ray looked back at the clearing where the orgy was still in full swing.

"Where's Jenny?" one of the guys shouted, "I got something large she can put in her mouth!" It was Mark Spock and he was his usual jovial self.

"Went for a piss Mr. Spock, probably passed out in the bushes," another biker retorted, "why don't you take you starship and go look for her?" Mark just laughed at the little joke and got up to go and look for Jenny to show her his large surprise.

"I will take this one," Cindy said softly. Ray and Jenny watched as she slowly made her way over to where the drunken biker entered the bushes to find Jenny. They only heard some muffled moans and then a tearing sound as Cindy's teeth sliced through the unlucky biker's flesh. It was only a few minutes later when Cindy returned with Mark Spock, the undead biker, following closely behind her. He had a large chunk of flesh missing from his upper arm and the cross around his neck looked somewhat out of place on his naked, overweight body.

"Now you and Jenny take the next one," Ray ordered as Mark and Jenny, the two newly crossed over members of the motorcycle club, looked at him expectantly. Cindy looked at Ray with approval and Ray realized that he had taken back full leadership of The Zombies. It may have been Cindy who had initiated the whole thing, but he was now fully back in charge and it felt good.

When one of the older men in the group wandered off into the bushes to relieve himself, Jenny and Mark made their way over to where they'd seen him entering the woods.

All of a sudden all hell broke loose and a series of terrible screams cut through the night.

"Get off me you motherfuckers! Aaargh!" the unfortunate biker screamed as Jenny and Mark jumped on top of him. They sank their eager teeth into him and ripped large pieces of flesh off his body while he was still alive.

Ray and Cindy rushed over to the place where the massacre was taking place and they were just in time to see Jenny and Mark finishing off the old geezer.

"Too late for this one," Cindy said and helped to drag the dead biker deep into the woods, whilst the rest of the drunken bikers stopped their sex orgy and shouted in highly concerned tones to find out what was going on.

"What the fuck! What are you doing over there!?"

The four Zombies kept dragging the old biker until they had his body about a hundred yards away from the clearing. Jenny and Mark immediately resumed their bloody feast and Cindy joined in by ripping some tasty flesh off the old guy's thigh. Ray found his own spot of delicious meat on the old biker's upper leg and within minutes the four undead bikers were looking down at the corpse of the old biker. His skeleton was clearly visible and there was no point in hanging a cross around his neck. There was no flesh left on his body to protect from the hungry undead.

"Now we've eaten well, from now on only one bite," Ray ordered and the undead bikers looked at him with slightly guilty expressions on their faces.

"Better hide, they're coming," Mark said as the voices of the rest of the bikers drew closer. They had a flashlight shining through the trees and it lent an eerie, unreal atmosphere to the dark woods.

There were still about ten bikers left who had not yet crossed over and it would take careful planning to get all of them, Ray thought as he led the other three to a particularly dark place amongst some dense growth.

"There's nothing here and I'm fucking scared," a young woman said in a high, shrill voice, "please come back to the camp with me?"

"I will go with you," a young biker suggested and they started making their way back to where the fire was still burning.

"Come, we will take the two of them together," Ray said and soon the four zombies were following closely on the tracks of the scared young girl and the guy who'd offered to take her back to the camp. The two bikers didn't even know what hit them and for once the undead bikers were somewhat disciplined, as they only took a single healthy bite out of each of the living before helping them to cross over.

"Here, this is yours. Don't ever take it off," Cindy said and hung a cross around each of the two new undead members' necks.

CHAPTER THREE

"Aaaaahhh!" someone screamed, terrified.

"Don't look at it," a man's voice spoke up and the rest of the bikers tried to tear their eyes away from the corpse of the old biker which was partially visible under a large bush. Parts of his skeleton showed through his ripped clothes which still clung to parts of his dead body.

"There must be some kind of lion or dangerous animal out here," Charlie Rickets suggested and this suggestion was quickly accepted by the rest of the group. It made sense and, even though the sight of the ripped up remains of the old biker had been terrible to behold, at least the thought of him meeting his end by means of a carnivorous wild animal brought the whole thing back to some level of natural explanation.

"Let's go back to the camp, we will come and bury him tomorrow," Charlie suggested and a quick consensus was reached that this was the best way to proceed.

"I still haven't seen Ray or Cindy and Jenny and Mark Spock are also missing," someone else spoke up and everyone looked around at the rest of the group as if they were hoping to see the missing bikers reappear magically in their midst.

"There's nothing we can do about it now, let's wait until morning and then we'll send out a search party," Charlie said in an authoritative voice.

"Can't we just drive the fuck out of this godforsaken place right now?" one of the younger girls asked with a pleading voice.

"There's no way we can drive anywhere tonight on our bikes. We're all pissed and it's just way too dangerous," Charlie said.

Everyone seemed to agree that this was true. The fact that Charlie Rickets had been sandwiched in between two naked biker chicks only half an hour earlier, whilst drinking whiskey from a bottle at the same time, didn't seem to be much of a concern to anyone. He'd taken over leadership in the absence of Ray Mason and was now looked up to for guidance out of this mess.

When the group arrived back at the camp they put some more wood on the fire and then all huddled close together to see out the night. Being a gang of drunken bikers, and not a well-organized group of military personnel out on a mission, no one thought that it might be a good idea to put out an alternating guard for the evening and soon everyone in the group was snoring away in a concerned, drunken slumber. From the darkness of the woods, six pairs of bloodshot eyes were looking at the group of sleeping bikers and the heavy breathing of the undead stalkers was the only thing that betrayed their impatience.

Suddenly the soft sounds of violin music penetrated the stillness of the night, as Cindy switched on her little radio.

One of the girls in the campsite got up in a half hypnotized state and started walking towards the sounds of music coming from the woods.

"Leave this one for me," Ray said and watched as the girl approached them. She was clearly sleepwalking, as her eyes were empty and she had no expression on her face. She came closer and closer and, finally, she was no more than ten feet away. The young girl walked right up to the end of the clearing and as Ray searched the dark recesses of his mind he could still remember her name through his fuzzy thoughts. Angelique...he couldn't quite remember her surname; he was more interested in finding put what her flesh tasted like. Hopefully, they could all control themselves and not rip her to shreds the way they'd done with the old guy.

Just as she was close enough for Ray to make his deadly move he froze in his tracks. She was wearing a cross around her neck and he was totally incapable of completing the deadly plan of attack he'd formed in his mind.

"Bad luck Ray," Cindy said as the girl walked back to where the rest of the bikers were sleeping.

"Where did you go off to, don't you know there's a dangerous animal out there somewhere?" a young biker asked as she lay down next to him.

"Had to go and see the music," Angelique replied and fell asleep almost immediately after saying that.

The young guy sat up straight and then he heard the music coming from the edge of the woods.

"Karl, wake up!" he said and shook another biker who was sleeping close by.

"What the fuck?" Karl said as he woke up and rubbed his eyes in disgust.

"Listen to that music," the young biker replied and Karl craned his neck to hear the sweet sounds coming out of the woods.

"Let's go and see where it's coming from," the young guy suggested and Karl, imagining how he would be admired by the rest of the bikers if he had a cool story to tell the next morning about finding the source of the music in the dark of the dangerous night, agreed to go and find out where the sounds were coming from.

They walked ever so slowly to the place where the radio was playing and the six undead bikers got ready.

"We need them to help fight so don't eat up," Ray said and the zombies nodded their heads slowly.

Karl and the young guy never saw what was coming until it was way too late. Three undead bikers jumped on each of them and, with surprising discipline, took small bites out of their flesh to help them across the river to the darkness of everlasting undead life.

Some of the bikers next to fire looked up from their drunken slumber to see where the rustling sounds and soft moans were coming from, but they were too late to see the end of two more men from their number.

"Now we are as many as they are," Ray said as eight pairs of undead eyes looked at the eight remaining bikers next to the fire.

"Get ready, we take them now before morning sun," Ray said and the other zombies looked at him with approval in their bloodied eyes.

"Attack!" Ray shouted in a terrible voice and the eight undead bikers rushed forward with surprising speed and landed upon the rest of the living members of The Zombies motorcycle club before anyone could even think of mounting a defense. Each undead zombie jumped on his own prey, except for Jenny, who was left staring at the cross dangling from Angelique's neck.

"Get away from me you monster!" Angelique shouted and held on to the cross when she saw Jenny staring at it with puzzled eyes.

"You're afraid of this, aren't you? You satanic piece of shit! I should have never let you talk me into coming here on this godforsaken trip!" Angelique screamed as the rest of the bikers were killed and turned into zombies right in front of her eyes.

"Why don't you take off that cross and join all of us?" Cindy said with blood dripping from her lips. Nineteen undead bikers stood together, all of them with their eyes fixed on Angelique.

Get away from me, just get away!" Angelique shouted through her tears and sent up a silent prayer, promising to mend her ways and to stay away from satanic biker gangs for the rest of her days, if only she was spared to survive that terrible night.

"We will wait until you fall asleep and take off the cross," Ray said with an ominous smile and the zombies retreated with him to the edge of the clearing to wait for Angelique to fall asleep.

They sat there staring at the only remaining living member of their motorcycle club, but Angelique never once lay down for the rest of the evening and she was still sitting up straight when the first rays of the morning sun broke through the trees to announce the arrival of a new day.

CHAPTER FOUR

"What the hell happened here?" Captain John Wesley asked with a deeply concerned tone in his voice as he helped Angelique O'Leary to her feet.

"Undead...all of them zombies," Angelique mumbled and the police psychiatrist scolded Captain Wesley for his harsh approach.

"Twenty of her friends are missing and she's been left alone here all night, you can't interrogate her that way!" Doctor Riley said as she draped a blanket over Angelique's shivering frame.

"Well there's a dead body lying a hundred yards from here under a bush and it's my job to find out what the hell caused him to meet his end that way. Looks like he's been eaten alive!" Captain Wesley said too loudly, before marching off in irritation while Doctor Riley offered Angelique some sugar water to help with the shock.

"Don't you worry dear," Doctor Riley said, "trust a bunch of bikers to run off and leave a young girl alone when there's a dangerous animal around!" she added and Angelique decided, right there and then, that this was going to be her official version of the events of the previous evening; that some animal had attacked the group and that they all drove off in a mad rush on their bikes, leaving her to fend for herself.

"Where do you want us to take you, my dear?" Doctor Riley asked, "Do you want to go to a hospital?"

"No, I want to go home to my parents," Angelique whispered while she clutched the cross that had saved her life, "I haven't seen them for nine months and I want to go to church with them again just like the old days."

"No problem, I will drive you home myself. And don't you worry about Captain Wesley, he can take your statement later," Doctor Riley said and helped Angelique into an official police vehicle.

CHAPTER FIVE

Nine motorcycles appeared on the horizon. Each was driven by a male biker and had a female on the back, clinging to the male body in front of her. Some of these bikers had chunks of their flesh missing, but this fact was obscured by the black leather outfits they were wearing. One or two members of The Zombies motorcycle club were missing some flesh from their faces, but these bikers simply never took off their helmets, even when The Zombies stopped along the way; like when they were hungry and needed a bite to eat.

Ray Mason was still their leader and, to be honest, he preferred the way things were after they had all crossed over to the other side. They no longer paid for things like gas and food. Gas was simply taken without payment. If anyone complained about it, they would become lunch or dinner for The Zombies.

The bikers found themselves somewhere on the dusty road between Spring Valley and Las Vegas and Ray slowed his motorcycle down to signal that they would be stopping at the roadside bar which had suddenly appeared out of nowhere.

When all of their motorcycles came to a roaring halt in front of the bar one or two of the patrons inside peered out the window to see what was going on.

"Who's making all that racket outside?" old Tom Barnett asked with a half drunk voice.

"Just some bikers Tom," the pretty bar lady answered and looked in the mirror behind the bar counter to adjust her blonde hair. It wasn't often they got so many visitors to the little bar all at once and, who knows, Mr. Right could still walk in there one day and save her from this dead end watering hole in the middle of the desert, Brenda thought as she smiled at herself in the mirror.

"How can I help you," she asked in her friendliest voice as an attractive blonde haired biker in his mid-thirties walked in next to a slutty woman with long black hair.

"Trust a slut like that to catch the pick of the litter," Brenda thought as she looked at the dark-haired female biker with poorly disguised animosity.

"Just want something to drink," the attractive young biker said, "and is there a police station nearby?"

He's not much of a conversationalist, Brenda thought, and there's something oddly incoherent in the way he speaks...but who cares, he's gorgeous and perhaps I can take him off that slut's hands by getting her all pissed or something.

"No cops around for miles so you can be just as bad as you want to be," she said and winked at the blonde biker. She really hoped that he was going to warm up a bit later. Perhaps she could offer him a couple shots of free Mexican Tequila to get his juices flowing.

"Why don't you invite all of your friends outside to come in too?" she asked, reasoning that it was best to hedge her bets and see if there wasn't perhaps some sexy young biker amongst the rest of the gang to take upstairs to her bedroom, just in case she couldn't manage to steal the blonde haired biker away from his girlfriend.

Old Tom Barnett looked outside with obvious anguish when Brenda suggested that the rest of the bikers should also enter the bar.

"Think I'll be leaving, for now," old Tom said and hurried out of the bar, leaving a half full glass of beer behind. He wasn't in the mood to find out what a bunch of drunken bikers had in mind for fun after a couple of stiff drinks. He also didn't like the cold calculated way the young biker and his girlfriend were looking around the bar as if they were planning a robbery or something.

"Did you hear that darling? We have the entire bar to ourselves and not a cop around for a hundred miles," the slutty biker chick said and the blonde guy almost smiled.

"I will get the others," the blonde biker announced and walked outside to get the rest of The Zombies.

"Are you thirsty my dear? I got some really strong Mexican tequila for you to try out," Brenda suggested and took an extra tall glass from the shelf before filling it to the brim with tequila. "Have to get her pissed as soon as possible to leave me the best possible chance to take the blonde guy off her hands," she thought as she pushed the glass of tequila across the bar counter.

"Thank you so much," the dark haired woman said as she picked up the glass of liquor. "Would you mind if I tried that on for a second?" she asked and pointed to the necklace the bar lady was wearing. It had a large cross dangling from a silver chain. Brenda had gotten it from her mother as a gift when she'd turned 21.

"I really can't take it off, I promised my mother I'd always wear it for good luck," Brenda answered as she held the cross between her fingers.

"Really? What if I did a good word for you with my brother, I saw the way you looked at him when we walked in," the dark haired woman said with a sly smile.

Brenda felt the excitement well up in her chest. So this woman wasn't competition for her at all; in fact, she could be the key to landing in the blonde biker's arms!

"Oh well, now that you put it that way...I guess you can try it on for a second," Brenda said and slowly took off her necklace before handing it to the dark haired woman.

"Thank you so much," the dark biker chick said and reached across the counter, "we're all dying of hunger."

Brenda looked at the swinging doors of the bar and the last thing she ever saw was the blonde man of her dreams leading a group of menacing looking bikers inside.

THE ZOMBIE EFFECT by Michael Bowen
Tuesday

"Another useless day," Jaime said as he turned the radio up.

The asshole behind him was honking his horn like Jaime could actually do anything about the endless row of cars in front of him.

"Yeah, we all have places to be, buddy!" he shouted at the rear-view mirror.

The asshole flashed him the finger, and Jaime could feel his face grow hot with anger. He almost reached for the door handle, but gripped the steering wheel tighter instead. Getting out of his car to have a screaming match with some penny pusher would make the day infinitely worse, and it was a shitter already.

The car in front of him moved about an inch forward, and the asshole behind him blared his horn again when Jaime didn't close the gap quick enough. He eased off the clutch of his 1969 Shelby Mustang and let her roll forward. He half expected the idiot behind him to ram the Jeep up his ass, but it looked like the driver was having a screaming match with his cell phone.

"What the hell is going on?" he shouted at the cars in front of him out of pure frustration.

He skipped through the channels on the radio, looking for a traffic report, or news report, or something to explain why he'd been wasting the last fifty minutes of his life staring at the same street in lower Manhattan.

"...in the central area. Motorists should remain calm and stay in their vehicles at all times."

"Remain calm, my ass," he snorted as he cast a quick glance at old horn-friendly behind him.

He jumped to another station.

"...today. Shots have been fired by the police, and all members of the public are advised to avoid Downtown Manhattan and the surrounding areas."

Jaime looked at his radio like it had grown human appendages. *Shots fired? At who?*

A loud tap on his window nearly made him lose his breakfast. Eggs and toast would not have looked great running down the front side of his suit.

"Hey, man," the teenager standing by his door shouted through the glass, "you know what's going on?"

Jaime rolled the window down.

"No idea," he replied, "I just heard some shit on the radio, gunshots or something Downtown."

"Freakin' terrorists, man," the teenager said, staring over the surrounding cars with that look of absolute knowing wisdom reserved for members of his age.

Jaime didn't reply.

"Hey, you got a smoke?" the teenager asked, shoulders suddenly hunched forward like he was doing a drug deal.

"Sorry, kid," Jaime replied, "I quit. You should, too."

The acne scars on the boy's face contorted slightly in a combination of disappointment and *what the hell do you know*? Jaime cringed on the inside. If he had given an adult that same look when he was this kid's age, he'd have gone to sleep with a broken rib and a busted lip. He was glad to see the little shit skulk away to bother someone else.

Fifteen minutes later and he had progressed about another two inches or so. Perfect. He couldn't wait to get to work to see his boss' bright red face explode in a flurry of spittle and curse words. It's not like Jaime had been working his ass off for the last six months, doing three people's jobs all by himself, right? The amount of time he spent at work was sickening. It really was true what they said – what's the use of having a lot of money if you never get to enjoy it? He suddenly appreciated being stuck in traffic if it meant he didn't have to be in his office.

Jaime's head shot up when heard someone scream.

The usual sounds of traffic surrounded him as he switched the radio off. Everything looked normal – people sitting in their cars, staring off into space with that special why-am-I-even-alive look in their eyes, kids in the back-seat texting or fighting with their siblings, women checking their make-up, a cabbie picking his nose. Was he the only one who heard it? The thought of imagining a thing like that caused a trickle of sweat to run down his back. The scream had sounded way too much like his sister, Claire. He'd often thought about how utterly messed up it was to know the sound of your sister's scream off by heart. Even now, fifteen years after he'd moved away from Redding Falls and all the memories embedded in its very streets, he sometimes still jerked awake at night in a cold sweat, Claire's screams ringing through his head like it was a bell tower. He couldn't deal with this shit now. He reached for the glove box and the serenely mind-numbing prescription meds within it, but stopped cold when he heard the scream again. This time he wasn't the only one. People got out of their cars to see what the commotion was about.

Jaime started to open his door but it was slammed shut again as the scar-faced teenager came sprinting down the street between the cars.

"Little shit," Jaime cursed.

He got out of his car and checked the side of the door for any scratches before staring angrily at the back of the kid's blazer.

The teenager turned his head for only a second, but what Jaime saw in his eyes made him whirl around in the direction from which he was running. More people were sprinting down the street, criss-crossing between the cars. Some were even running *over* the cars. The screams were louder now. Maybe there really *were* terrorists.

Jaime looked around nervously. The people around him were succumbing to that primal instinct which demands that you run when you see other members of your species run. The occupant in the Jeep behind him was still screaming into his cell phone, though, blissfully unaware that people were abandoning their cars and making a break for it.

Jaime stood rooted to the hot pavement. His legs were practically vibrating, itching to be off. The primal instinct wasn't lost on him, but the thought of leaving the car he'd basically built from the ground up just sitting in the street while God knows what had its violent way with it, suppressed mother nature for the time being.

The sound of gunshots was getting louder now. Warm bodies shoved past him on their way to safety. He tried to ask a few of them what the hell was going on, but either they didn't know, or didn't feel that he needed to know. Some of the people streaming past him had bloody faces and torn clothes, their faces fixed in an expression of perpetual shock.

"I'll be coming back for you, baby," he said to the car as he grabbed his briefcase from the back-seat.

He cast another quick glance in the direction from which everyone was running. A policeman was running down the narrow lane created by the cars on either side.

"Officer, what's..."

Jaime's words died on his lips as a woman tackled the policeman from behind. The cop's face smashed into the road as his gun slid over the tar and came to a rest at Jaime's feet. The woman was writhing on the cop's back like she was doing a mechanical bull ride. The noises coming out of her mouth were nightmare inducing, reminding Jaime of the sounds his grandfather had made just before he died of lung cancer. In one horrific motion, the woman slammed her face into the cop's neck, causing him to scream out in pain. He clawed at the tar beneath him, reaching out to Jaime with fierce desperation.

This can't be real, Jaime thought as the woman's teeth ripped chunk after chunk of flesh from the cop's neck. Her face and hands were covered in the blood streaming out of the wound.

The eggs and toast he had for breakfast ended up on the front side of his suit after all. A moment of clear thought dedicated to self-preservation made Jaime pick up the gun lying by his feet before he ran for his life.

Wednesday

"Mom, pick up the goddamned phone!" Jaime screamed at his mother's voice mail before flinging his cell phone onto the bed.

He shoved more things into an open backpack, his brain frantically trying to think of items he couldn't do without. It disturbed him to think that the first thing he threw into the bag as soon as he made up his mind to go check on his mom, was the bottle of pills he'd come to rely on so much the last couple of years. But he needed them, now more than ever. The world was going to shit around him, and he couldn't deal with it by himself. In fact, there were lots of things he couldn't deal with by himself, and most of them were in Redding Falls. Christ knows why he was racing to get back there – he didn't even know whether his mom was home or not.

A few minutes later he was roaring down the littered street on his dad's 1981 Harley Davidson, the only good thing he'd ever gotten from the man. At first he thought he'd be able to head back into the city to get his pride and joy from where she was sitting pretty in the street, but after the news reports, helicopters, fires and riots from the previous night, he'd made peace with the fact that he would probably never see the car again. The only thing anyone knew for sure, was that some sort of virus had broken out in the city – a virus which seemed to turn people into crazed lunatics. The actual word *zombie* wasn't mentioned, but Jamie wasn't an idiot. He knew what he saw in the street the day before wasn't just some woman with a swollen brain or something. She'd been *eating* that cop like he was a buffet dinner. And from what he could tell from the constant news reports, the cop hadn't been the only victim. Not by a long shot.

To be honest, there were worse ways to get out of town. All four lanes of the highway were stuffed full of cars stuffed full of people, but the bike whizzed past in the emergency lane. Sirens were blaring somewhere in the distance, but Jaime honestly didn't give a shit about road rules anymore. That damned car was the only reason he hadn't bugged out of there the day before already, and he was itching to be as far away from the city as possible.

He had to do some off-roading as he approached the apparent cause of the traffic jam – four cars were overturned, blocking all the lanes. Jaime tried not to look at the bodies lying in the road, especially the ones who didn't look like they had gotten there because of the accident. Ambulances and police cars were parked next to the road, but no one slowed or stopped him as he wound his way through them. After that, the highway was just an empty stretch of asphalt under the scorching sun.

Thursday

Jaime rapped his knuckles on the screen door before ringing the doorbell for the hundredth time.

"Mom?" he called.

No one answered. The house was locked up tight, mail piled on the "Welcome to our Home" matt. *Home indeed,* Jaime thought a bit disdainfully as he glanced around at the brightly painted flower pots and the spotless white walls. The house had never looked like this while he was growing up. Back then it had been a shit hole, the screen door dirty and broken, the windows unwashed, dog shit on the front lawn, motor oil staining the driveway – all the things which disappeared as his mom rebuilt her life after Jaime Snr was finally locked up. He knew his mom still missed his dad, even if she would never admit it to anyone, especially not her new husband. His dad was a drunk, and a violent one at that. The only people who suffered under his fist more than his mother did, had been Jaime and his sister. But his mom had that incomprehensible affliction most women in abusive marriages seemed to suffer from – she always protected the son of a bitch. Even when he had beaten Jaime half to death for skipping school, or when he had broken Claire's arm after he caught her making out with a boy behind the shed. His mom just cried, and told the kids to be quiet, to go to their rooms, to go to sleep, to stop crying. Everything was always hushed up, swept under the rug with all the other garbage littering the place. It had been the story of her life. It wasn't the first time Jaime wondered if his mom blamed herself for what happened to Claire. He knew he definitely blamed himself for it.

He waited another few minutes before getting back on the bike and heading into town. The same old run-down buildings of Redding Falls were baking in the heat of the midday sun, their paint peeling off like they were melting. There were no manicured lawns here, only weeds and dirt and junk. Jaime knew all the secret places, all the spots you could get away from the sun, or hide from your drunk father and his buddies. He hadn't been into the town proper in well over fifteen years, and God knew he hadn't missed the place.

He pulled into Joe's parking lot and pulled the keys from the bike's ignition. For a while he just sat on the motorcycle's roasting leather seat, sweat running into his eyes. If there was anyone who knew where his mom was, it was Joe, but his bar was the local watering hole for all the assholes Jaime had had the displeasure of sharing a high school with. He felt just like a kid again, sitting there, baking in the sun, not sure why he was afraid of going into the dark dingy interior of the bar. He thought he'd left all this shit behind, including his sense of worthlessness. But your past has a way of sneaking up on you, yelling *surprise!* and punching you in the gut.

He could feel the heat coming off of the pavement as he made his way to the bar's entrance. The iconic rock 'n roll music was streaming through the door in an incoherent garble of noise.

It was the middle of the week, the middle of the day, but the bar was packed. In a small town like Redding Falls, drinking was the only thing to do to pass the time. If you didn't drink, you didn't belong. Jaime forced himself to walk straight to the counter. He didn't so much as glance around to see whether he recognized any of the faces.

"Jaime!" Joe called as soon as he spotted him.

Jaime smiled in spite of himself. Joe had always been a massive man, but Jaime remembered him to be taller, more intimidating. He seemed to have aged a hundred years since the last time Jaime saw him.

"Hey, Joe," he said as he shook the barkeep's hand over the polished counter.

"Look at you!" Joe said, throwing his hands into the air, "It's been, what, ten years?"

"Fifteen," Jaime replied, shifting his feet uncomfortably.

The bar had gotten a lot quieter since he walked in. He still refused to look around.

"What brings you back home, kid?" Joe asked.

"My mom," Jaime replied, "Any idea where she is?"

"Yeah, sure," Joe ran a hand through his gray and thinning hair, "Her and Ted went down to Jill's a couple weeks ago. I've been checking on the house every now and then. They should be back on Sunday."

"Thanks, Joe," Jaime said and turned to go.

"Hey, Jaime, you hear about what's been happening up in the cities? You live in New York now, don't you?" Joe asked before he could walk away.

The bar fell completely silent. Jaime could feel everyone's eyes on him. He wished he could slither out of there like a damned snake.

"Some kind of virus," he cleared his throat, images of that woman gorging herself on the cop's flesh flashing through his mind, "It's not safe there."

"What's the government doing?" someone asked from the other side of the room.

"Probably nothing, as usual," someone else answered him.

Questions and answers were shot back and forth across the place as Jaime retreated back into the blinding heat of the day. He was just about to start the bike back up again when Joe came running across the parking lot.

"Jaime, wait up," he wheezed, wiping his face with the cloth he used to keep the counter so nice and shiny.

"Don't hurt yourself, Joe," Jaime said, not unkindly.

"Jaime, listen…" Joe took a few seconds to catch his breath, "The reason Florence is outta town… It's your dad, Jaime. He was released early. He's been back a couple weeks."

For all the heat of the day, Jaime's blood still ran cold. He stared at Joe, unable to even fathom a reply. His dad, out of prison, and in Redding Falls. What were the odds?

"He's staying at Marcy's," Joe said, even though Jaime hadn't asked.

The Harley roared to life.

"Stock up on some supplies," Jaime said as he fastened his helmet, "You know, water, food, fuel. I think shit's going to get ugly with this virus."

He sped down the road, unsure if it was sweat or tears running into his eyes.

Sunday

Jaime let the curtain of his motel room fall into place again. For the third time that morning he saw a loaded up truck speed down the road.

Where are they even going? he wondered. People from the city fled to towns, people from the towns fled to smaller towns, people from the smaller towns fled to even smaller towns, and people from even smaller towns fled to places like Redding Falls. Where the hell did people from Redding Falls go?

The small and nearly useless TV sitting on the cabinet next to the bed was on mute, but Jaime didn't need to hear anything to know what was going on. The virus had spread rapidly. It was spreading over the entire country like some massive brooding storm. People were dying in drones, but they weren't staying down. Nope, they got right back up a few hours later. Only, they weren't the same. For one, they seemed to lose all manner of coherent speech. Oh, and they seemed to have an insufferable craving for human flesh. Zombies. People were finally beginning to use the damn term. None had been spotted in Redding Falls yet, though. Well, at least none that Jaime had heard of, but it wasn't like he was socializing with the locals. He'd been keeping to himself, waiting for his mom to get back so they could plan their next move together. *She might not even be coming back,* he thought. If he had known that his dad had been released early, he sure as hell wouldn't have set a damn foot in this shit hole, no matter what manner of undead things were chasing him.

He packed up his stuff and headed back to his mom's place. He was feeling paranoid and on edge. Every person in the street looked like his dad. Jaime didn't know what he would do if he came face to face with the bastard. The gun he had picked up back in the streets of Manhattan suddenly felt like it weighed a hundred pounds in his backpack, but it made him feel better. Even if he never pulled the trigger, he would still love the opportunity to point it at his dad's face.

Jaime noticed Ted's car in the driveway as he pulled up to his mom's house. Florence came running through the front door, her face knotted in concern. He could see from the bags under her eyes that she'd been crying.

"Jaime!" she shouted as she ran up the sidewalk.

"Hey, mom," he said as she threw her arms around his neck.

Her back was bonier than he remembered, but she still wore the same perfume he remembered from when he was a kid. Some things never changed. He suddenly felt like vermin for not visiting her more often. It took him a moment to realize that she was crying on his shoulder.

"Mom, what's wrong?" he asked, holding her away from him to get a better look at her.

Mascara was running down her cheeks. She seemed so unlike the woman who had raised him.

"It's Ted," she sobbed, "He's hurt, Jaime. Something horrible happened. Your aunt is dead."

He crushed her to his chest again and stroked her hair, trying to soothe her but unsure of what to say. His aunt Jill was much older than his mom, and she had been struggling with cancer for years. The news wasn't altogether surprising.

"Mom, where's Ted?" he asked when the sobs subsided.

"The bedroom," she said shakily, taking a deep breath and putting her nothing-is-wrong-anymore face on. *There she is,* Jaime thought bitterly.

The bedroom was dark and stuffy, the curtains drawn against the harsh glare of sunlight streaming through the windows. Ted was lying on top of the covers, his face drenched in a sticky and unhealthy looking sweat. His breaths were short and shallow, and his eyelids kept fluttering open like he was on a bad acid trip.

"What happened?" Jaime asked as he sat down next to him.

He pressed the back of his hand to Ted's forehead, expecting it to be scalding hot, but it was ice cold.

"Your aunt Jill," his mom began, her voice on the verge of cracking again, "She came home one day with this... this wound on her arm. She said someone at the bank attacked her. She said he... he *bit* her, Jaime! She got so ill, just like... just like Ted. She died, during the night. We didn't know. The next morning, Ted went into her room and found her. She was dead, Jaime. I felt for a pulse. She was dead! But, a short while later, while we were waiting for the ambulance, she... she came back to life. But she... she was so much stronger than she had ever been. And the noises she made... We didn't know what to do. Ted tried to calm her down, to get her back into bed, but she attacked him. She was like an animal! Whatever it was, she wasn't my sister anymore. She bit him, Jaime!"

Jaime felt his stomach sink lower and lower with each word which came out of her mouth.

"And now, Ted is like this, and…"

"Mom," he interrupted her, "be quiet for a moment."

She shut her mouth with the trained precision you could only get from having been married to a bully. Jaime knew it well because he had it too.

He looked at Ted's paling face. Blue vines were criss-crossing over his cheeks and nose like his skin was becoming thinner and thinner.

"Show me where she bit him," he told Florence as he went over to her.

"Ted, honey," she said softly and soothingly, "Jaime is here, he's going to take a look, okay?"

If Ted heard or understood what was happening around him, he gave no indication. He wasn't dead yet, Jaime could see his heart racing in his throat.

Florence rolled him onto his side, revealing a bloody soaked rag stuck to his left shoulder. Jaime stepped closer for a better look but regretted it as a sickening stench washed over him. She removed the cloth, holding her breath, probably to stop herself from retching. Jaime felt the color drain from his face when he saw the bite mark. The wound was massive and bloody, and it looked badly infected. The skin around the teeth marks was black like he had gotten frost bite or something.

"Mom," Jaime said as she put a fresh cloth on Ted's shoulder and eased him back onto the bed, "This is bad."

She didn't answer him. She just kept patting Ted's face with a wet cloth, soothing him with soft words. Jaime left the room and its stench for the cooler and better smelling kitchen. Everything in the house was different, all the old furniture had been sold or simply carted off to the dump. The photographs of him and Claire were the only things in the house which reminded him of the life he had there while growing up.

He couldn't look at the photos, though. Fifteen years after his sister died, and the wound felt as fresh as the one on Ted's shoulder.

"Your father got released early, you know," his mom said from behind him as he was pouring himself a glass of water.

"Ted's going to die, mom," he said simply.

"I know, Jaime," she replied softly, "I know."

Monday

The power went out that morning. Afterwards, Jamie wondered if he would ever have known what was happening upstairs if the power hadn't cut out exactly when it did. His life was beginning to seem like a series of strange coincidences, one shit event leading to the next even shittier one.

He was watching the news, trying to figure out where, if anywhere at all, the virus hadn't managed to spread yet. He wanted to get his mom out of town before Ted died, or rather before he woke up again. The broadcaster was just repeating the same bulletins over and over again, though, like the whole bloody world had gotten stuck on the same bit of information.

The TV suddenly died, plunging the whole house into silence. A soft shuffling noise was coming from the room above him – his mom's bedroom.

"Mom?" he called nervously.

He had expressly forbidden her from going into the room without him. It was too damn risky. Christ only knew when Ted would finally shove of his mortal coil for a flashier, deadlier version.

He took the stairs slowly, straining his ears for any new sounds. More shuffling, more moving about.

"Mom?" he called again, unnerved by the fear he heard in his own voice.

The bedroom door was closed, but his mom was nowhere to be seen. He pressed his ear to the door and heard more shuffling from within. *This can only be bad, or really, really bad,* he thought.

If he'd been smarter he would have gotten the gun from his bag, or he would have at least gotten one of Ted's golf clubs from the garage. But concern for his mom and what might be happening to her seemed to make him a little bit stupid, kind of like when he was standing in the middle of the street while everyone around him was running away because he didn't want to leave his damned car behind.

He turned the knob as softly as he possibly could. The door swung open silently, revealing the hellish scene within. The white carpet, curtains, and walls were covered in dark red blotches. Florence was lying on the floor. Looming over her, his face pressed to her chest, was Ted, or whatever remained of Ted. His mom's eyes were staring into the nothingness of death, her face fixed in an almost serene expression of complete oblivion. Her head rolled from side to side a bit every time Ted lifted his mouth from her body. A distant part of Jaime wondered if she had tried to call out to him before she died.

The slurping, sucking and chewing noises Ted was making as he ripped into his mother's flesh nearly made Jaime puke. As if his mouth wasn't enough of a weapon, Dead-Ted was using his nails to claw at her stomach, peeling off layer after layer of skin to get to what was inside her.

Jaime felt a sickening rage he had never known before. His mother was dead. His father was free, and his mother was dead. Ted was dead. Ted was *eating* his mother. The edges of his vision were beginning to grow dark.

"Get off her you fucking bastard!" he screamed and ran across the room.

Dead-Ted lifted his head in a confused daze before Jaime shoved him off of his mom's body and into the side of the bed. He wasn't down for long though, and came lurching at Jaime as soon as he got to his feet. Dead-Ted's eyes were a sickly yellow color, devoid of all traces of life or humanity. He was making those same disgusting noises the woman riding the mechanical bull-cop had made.

"Get the fuck away from me!" Jaime screamed as he shoved at Dead-Ted again.

But Dead-Ted wasn't Ted anymore. He was Ted 2.0, much stronger, much sturdier than the old man had been. He grabbed Jaime's arm in a steely grip, and before Jaime could even try and snatch it back again, he felt the searing pain of teeth ripping into his skin.

Tuesday

"Another useless day," Jaime said as he stumbled through the cemetery.

He was horribly drunk and in horrible pain.

"You know what," he said to the bottle of Jack Daniels clutched in his good hand, "I don't remember where she was buried. Isn't that fucking *weird*?"

He wound his way through the gravestones, much as he wound his way through traffic just a week before in Lower Manhattan. That part of the world seemed light years away. Now he was in Redding Falls, probably the most useless town which had ever existed in the history of towns, drunk out of his mind despite the one promise he had made himself fifteen years earlier to never *ever* get drunk again, a chunk of his arm was missing and probably rotting inside the stomach of the man who had brutally killed his mother, and he was trying to find the grave of his sister, who, fifteen years ago, was savagely beaten to death by his father. Oh yeah, life was *fucked up*.

The sun was already low in the sky by the time he finally found it.

In loving memory of Claire Michaels,
Loving daughter and sister, always remembered, always loved.

Jaime stared at the words for what seemed like hours. For the first time since she died, he allowed the memories of his sister to wash over him unchecked. She'd been such a bombshell with her blonde hair and green eyes. She made all the guys swoon like a bunch of idiots. But she was never a slut, she never led any of them on. She was what Jaime thought of as the purest shit under the sun. Her smile could make your head explode. But above all, she was kind. Older than Jaime by five years, he shuddered to think of what life must have been like for her before he was born, with no one else to soak up some of their father's thrashings.

He took another swig of the whiskey, not even feeling the burn in his throat anymore. He had started to sweat the same sickly sticky sweat he'd seen on Ted. He knew he didn't have much longer. But he'd be damned if he was gonna skulk through town like a damned brainless eating machine only to kill some granny hiding in her house. He still had the gun, and he was planning on using it on himself to end it all.

He read the inscription over and over again, tears rolling down his cheeks.

"Loved by all," he snorted, "Loved by all!"

He threw the empty bottle at the gravestone, sending shards of glass flying in every direction.

"She wasn't loved by all, you fucking liars!" he shouted, "She wasn't loved by the one man who was supposed to protect her!"

He fell onto his knees next to the stone, not caring that the pieces of broken bottle were digging into his skin. He clung to the gravestone like it was Claire. He so desperately wanted it to be Claire.

"I'm so sorry," he whimpered, "Claire, I'm so sorry... I should never have left you alone with him. I was such a stupid asshole! I knew what he was like. I knew... Please, Claire, please forgive me. Forgive your baby brother..."

His tears rolled down the as he cried with his face pressed to it. All the pain and anger he had kept so well under control for the past fifteen years just came streaming out of him. His skin was ice cold, but inside of him it felt like the fires of hell were raging in a relentless battle with whatever the virus was doing to him.

In his mind's eye, he saw his sister's face, again and again. So often she would stay home from school because of a busted lip or a bruised cheek. So often he would hear her cry out when his dad was feeling particularly irate, just as she must have heard him cry out too. They became each other's rocks, confiding in each other, cleaning the wounds, bandaging the limbs, stitching the cuts. She was his best friend, and he left her at home that night, alone, so that he could go out drinking with his friends, just like his dad would go out drinking with his. He left her, and the next time he saw her she was lying dead in a puddle of her own blood on the kitchen floor, her hair red instead of blonde.

"You bastard," he whispered as he saw his dad's face flash before his eyes, "You sick, twisted fucking bastard."

He stumbled back to the road and allowed his feet to carry him to what he knew would be his death.

Marcy's house was dark and silent as he walked up the cobbled steps to the front door. Would he knock? *Can I borrow a cup of sugar?* he thought, laughing out loud despite the seething anger he felt right down to his very soul.

"Who's there?" he heard the familiar voice call from inside the house.

The sound of it was somehow even worse than the sounds Dead-Ted had made.

"It's me, dad," he replied, trying to keep the contempt out of his voice but failing, "It's Jaime."

Footsteps. The lock on the door clicked, and suddenly Jaime was face to face with the monster under his bed, the villain in every nightmare, his father.

"Jaime," his dad said, surprised, "What... What are you doing here?"

"Shut up," Jaime said, pleased to see the color drain out of his dad's cheeks.

"What did you say?" he knew that tone all too well – it was the you-better-shut-your-mouth-right-now-or-I'm-gonna-break-your-teeth tone.

"I said, shut up!" he shoved his dad back into the house, half expecting the same resistance he got from Dead-Ted.

But his dad was fat and soft, and totally caught off guard. He fell back onto the floor.

"Jaime, what the..."

"I told you to *shut* up," Jaime said as he took the gun from the waistband of his jeans.

He'd only ever fired a gun at the gun range before, but he knew where to aim. His dad's face paled even more.

"Not very nice, is it?" Jaime asked, "Being trapped on the floor, cornered by someone stronger than you."

Jaime Snr didn't reply.

"You know, you should have rotted in prison. You should have died behind bars for what you did to her."

"Son, I..."

"Do *not* call me son, *ever*!"

Jaime's head was beginning to swim. He was feeling very drowsy like he could fall asleep right then and there. His dad must have seen his momentary lapse in concentration, because he got onto his feet and made a lunge for the gun. But Jaime had remembered how his dad's mind worked. He knew that you were at your most vulnerable around the man when you were distracted.

He pulled the trigger.

The gunshot ripped through the silence of the night.

The bullet hit his dad in the chest. He fell backward again, screaming out in pain as a thin streak of blood ran down his shirt.

Jaime could barely hang on to consciousness. He had half a clip left, but he suddenly felt like the crying pile of shit which was his father didn't deserve to be put out of his misery quite yet. His vision was darkening, the room swam before his eyes.

"No one's coming to help you," he managed to say, "You're going to die, just like she died. Scared, and alone."

Jaime pressed the gun to his temple and whispered one final repentance before pulling the trigger.

"Claire, I'm sorry."